"It's clearly important to you that I find some way for you to pay back that money."

"You've found some work for me?"

He smiled. "I've found a job for you—if you're willing to do it."

"I've told you, I'm prepared to do anything legal."

"Oh, this is legal," he assured her. Then evenly he enquired, "How would you like to be my steady girlfriend for a year?"

Merren stared at him. "You're not serious?"

"I promise you I am."

"But—but—we don't even know each other!" she protested.

"We don't have to—it will be an in-name-only courtship."

Jessica Steele lives in a friendly English village with her super husband, Peter. They are owned by a gorgeous Staffordshire bull terrier called Florence, who is boisterous and manic, but also adorable. It was Peter who first prompted Jessica to try writing and, after the first rejection, encouraged her to keep on trying. Luckily, with the exception of Uruguay, she has so far managed to research inside all the countries in which she has set her books, traveling to places as far apart as Siberia and Egypt. Her thanks go to Peter for his help and encouragement.

Books by Jessica Steele

HARLEQUIN ROMANCE®
3588—THE FEISTY FIANCÉE
3615—BACHELOR IN NEED
3627—MARRIAGE IN MIND

Don't miss any of our special offers. Write to us at the following address for information on our newest releases.

Harlequin Reader Service
U.S.: 3010 Walden Ave., P.O. Box 1325, Buffalo, NY 14269
Canadian: P.O. Box 609, Fort Erie, Ont. L2A 5X3

THE BACHELOR'S BARGAIN
Jessica Steele

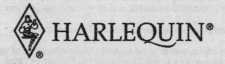

TORONTO • NEW YORK • LONDON
AMSTERDAM • PARIS • SYDNEY • HAMBURG
STOCKHOLM • ATHENS • TOKYO • MILAN • MADRID
PRAGUE • WARSAW • BUDAPEST • AUCKLAND

ISBN 0-373-03643-4

THE BACHELOR'S BARGAIN

First North American Publication 2001.

Visit us at www.eHarlequin.com

Printed in U.S.A.

CHAPTER ONE

MERREN tried to look on the bright side—or even find a bright side. By nature she was a cheerful person, but just lately there had been little to cheer about.

Looking on the bright side, however, she had the money in her bag which would take the look of strain from the face of Robert, her brother. It had been extremely disappointing that the sale of her mother's sapphire and diamond ring hadn't fetched anywhere near its insurance valuation. But the two thousand pounds she had been forced to accept was just enough to keep the bailiffs from Robert's door. Though since six weeks ago Robert, his wife and their three children had moved into the house she already lived in, it was her door too.

Not that he and his family didn't have a right to live there as well, Merren reminded herself as, having delivered an envelope in the area, she made her way past elegant and expensive houses *en route* to public transport.

It had to be today that Robert had wanted to borrow her car to go for a job interview. Though, she acknowledged, in the last six weeks it had become more like the family's car, rather than belonging exclusively to her. But Robert's need was greater than hers, and if he was successful at his interview, a company car, as in his old job, went with the territory.

Just as it had to be today that Robert's need of a car was greater than her own, it had to be today that her boss, Dennis Chapman, 'up to his eyes in it', to use his expression, had asked if she'd mind dropping some urgent documents off to one of his business associates on her way home. She had done so once before, and Dennis had obviously assumed she'd had her car outside today.

Merren's thoughts went back to her brother as she reflected on the mess he was in. If only he'd told someone a year ago that he'd been made redundant they might, collectively, have been able to find some way out of his problems. But he hadn't told anyone—not even his wife!

True, Carol, a terminal worrier at the best of times, had been four months pregnant with their third child then. But even so, though Robert had thought he'd get another job straight away, Merren felt sure that, had Carol known, she would have pulled with him rather than against him, as was happening now.

A year ago they could have... Merren's breath caught, the sadness she was having to come to terms with coming over her. A year ago her mother had been alive. A year ago she and her mother had lived happily together in the house Merren's father still owned. Ten months ago her mother had been out walking when a car coming round a sharp bend had gone out of control. It...

Merren turned her thoughts away from the shock and horror of that devastating time after her mother's death. She had valued Robert's support in the background then. But, aside from her love for her brother, Merren saw it as only right and natural that now, in his time of need, she should support him.

Their father lived in Cornwall, but, since he hadn't stirred himself to attend his estranged wife's funeral, they hardly expected any help from him in this financial crisis. Although before Robert had told Carol that their small savings were gone, that he hadn't been paying the mortgage and that they were soon to be homeless, he had written a number of times to his father for help—so far, he had received no reply.

Merren was deep in thought, and was passing one of the tall, imposing houses, when a young man in his early twenties came galloping out down the steps, a travel bag in his hand, and only just avoided cannoning into her.

'Sorry!' he called, his eyes appreciative of her face and figure.

He was soon from her mind and Merren walked on. She must get home. She didn't think Robert had told Carol that she was going to try to sell their mother's— and, before her, their grandmother's—ring. But he would be waiting. She must get home. She must...

All thought suddenly ceased when what happened next happened so fast she could hardly believe it was happening at all. One moment she was stepping purposefully out on the hard pavement; the following she was being pushed violently from behind—and the pavement was coming up to meet her.

Even while it was dawning on her that she was being mugged, three adrenalin-activated youths were pushing and shoving and hitting and generally making short work of her grim determination to hang on to her shoulder bag at all costs, and were escaping pell-mell down the road with it.

Feeling stunned and winded, it was the violence of the assault that shocked her. She had never ever been hit before and she just sat there dishevelled and decidedly crumpled for ageless seconds, dazed, sickened, a cross between tears and fury.

She did not cry, and there was no one there on whom she could vent her anger. How could she have been hit, pushed, knocked over in this salubrious area? Why not?

What better place for a mugging than this well-to-do district? What better place for rich pickings.

'Oh, you poor thing!' So dazed and in shock was she, Merren hadn't heard the sound of running feet; feet running towards her, not away. She looked up and recognised the young man who'd been carrying the travel bag out to his car. 'Can you stand up?' he asked, his face showing his concern.

Merren, with his aid, got to her feet; it was incidental that there were great gaping holes in her tights. Everything seemed to spin about her for a second, so she was glad when the man held on to her.

'Oh, you poor, poor thing,' he crooned. 'Those thugs will be miles away by now. Come on,' he urged. 'A cup of tea's what you need.'

With his hand under her arm supporting her he took the short way to a house where the front door still stood open. He helped her up the steps and Merren went with him.

A few minutes later she came a little out of her shock to find she was seated in someone's plush drawing room with barely any idea of how she had got there.

Her head had started to pound when a voice, somewhere to the back of her, started to penetrate. 'Not another of your waifs and strays, Piers!' It was rather a nice voice. Piers, whoever he was, apparently went in for collecting waifs and strays.

'Aw, don't be like that, Jarad, the poor girl's just been mugged!'

Merren jerked upright on the sofa she found herself on. They were talking about her! Waif and stray! Indignantly she went to stand up—her legs were wobbly; she sat down again. 'So had the last one been mugged, if I recall correctly.'

'It's true this time. Honestly, it is.'

'You haven't time to plead your case. You'll miss your plane.' The voices were moving away, the Piers voice mumbling something, then the Jarad voice answering, 'Yes, yes, I'll look after her—don't I always?'

Merren made a more determined effort to get herself together. Huh, waif and stray! Look after her—he could go take a hike. But her head hurt, her shoulders hurt, and she had an idea she'd have a few bruises by tomorrow. In fact her head felt a bit muzzy, but she'd stand up in a minute and get out of there.

She could hear some sort of a conversation going on, then silence. Then she heard a car start up. Good, they'd gone out somewhere. She heard the front door close, and, as a second or two afterwards someone came into the drawing room, Merren decided it was time to leave.

Just as she went to struggle to her feet, though, a tall man with night-black hair, somewhere in his mid-thirties, came and stood in front of her, and she found herself pinned by what she could only describe as a pair of cool grey eyes. He certainly wasn't going to believe a word she said, she could tell that, and that was before she so much as opened her mouth.

Which was why she decided that she wasn't going to bother saying anything. Though, since he was standing so close, she had to amend that decision. 'If you wouldn't mind getting out of my way, I'll leave.'

She hated his cynical right eyebrow that lifted at her haughty tone. 'You're different; I'll say that for you,' he drawled.

'I'm certainly no "waif or stray"!' she told him snappily. Though if she'd hoped to embarrass him by tossing back at him the words she'd overheard, she could have saved herself the bother.

He did not look a scrap embarrassed, nor in the slightest apologetic when he apologised dryly, 'Forgive me. I find it a trifle tedious being left to care for the lame dogs my brother constantly brings home—then, when his Samaritan impetuosity wanes, leaves me to deal with his problems.'

Problems! Lame dogs! Of all the insufferable... 'You miserable worm!' she flared. 'I was mugged!'

The epithet about the miserable worm didn't touch him, either. 'Very conveniently mugged on my doorstep,' he drawled, giving no quarter for her ruined tights and dishevelled appearance.

But she'd had it with him. Abruptly, too abruptly, she shot to her feet. She took one step, and as waves of dizziness assaulted her she needed something to hang on to. She stretched out her hands and held on to him until her world righted itself.

'I'm sorry,' she mumbled from a proud somewhere, dropping her hands from his arms as if burned, going to take another step. Only this time he held both of her arms and pushed her back to the sofa.

'Stay there,' he ordered, and, while every instinct in her urged her to tell him what he could do with his orders, she was feeling too drained just then to do anything other than obey.

He went away, but returned in seconds with a glass of medicinal brandy. 'Drink that,' he commanded, and, at her belligerent look that said, Why should I? he flicked a glance over her shoulder-length natural blonde-streaked pale reddish hair, over her fine features and porcelain skin, and commented, 'It could be that you're naturally pale, but...'

'Don't bust a gut giving me the benefit of the doubt!' Her spirit was returning—she felt better sitting down.

'Just as it could be that you're naturally lippy.'

'It's not every day I get mugged and then, while I'm coping with that, get accused of pretending to be mugged, for some reason my head's in too much of a fog just now to be able to work out why.'

'Drink the brandy.'

She tossed him a malevolent look, but, since it seemed the brandy might make her feel better, she took a sip, determined not to choke on the unfamiliar spirit, and took another couple of sips—whereupon her determination not to choke let her down. But only so far as a lady-like splutter.

She did, however, acknowledge, albeit reluctantly, that she was starting to recover from the shock and humiliation of being set upon by a trio of thugs.

'Drink the rest of it and I'll get a taxi to take you home,' the man Jarad said.

A taxi—to Surrey! 'I haven't the money for a tax...' Aghast, she stopped, fresh shock hitting her as, looking round for her bag, suddenly she fully remembered that the last time she had seen it some young thug was making off with it. 'The money!' she gasped in horror, she'd had two thousands pounds in that bag!

'Here we go!' drawled the man Jarad nastily. And, as Merren stared blankly at him, 'Would it be very impolite of me, do you suppose, if I enquire what money?'

Merren had grown up loving her fellow man, but she had just come across one that she most definitely hated. She, who hadn't a violent bone in her body, and maybe because of the violence recently done to her, felt she wanted to thump him, to hit him and keep on hitting him. But she had been better brought up than that. But her tone was full of loathing when she placed the brandy glass down on a nearby table and told him coldly, 'Never, have I ever met a more odious creature than you.'

'My heart bleeds—how much will it cost me?'

You'd have thought someone would have bashed that good-looking face in before this! 'You—nothing.'

'Let me try again. How much did the muggers get away with?'

Merren doubted that he'd decided to believe she'd been mugged after all. But pride about letting him know that she wasn't the penniless 'waif and stray' he seemed so convinced she was made her answer, 'Two thousand pounds, actually.'

'In cash?' She refused to answer. 'You usually carry that amount of cash around with you?' he questioned sceptically.

'It was to pay some bills!' Why did she feel she had to defend herself? She was going—getting out of there.

'You don't have a chequebook?' he asked, before she had moved an inch.

She didn't have two thousand in her account, nor even a quarter of that. Nor was she likely to tell him that Robert's creditors had point-blank told him that a cheque would be unacceptable. Merren could only suppose he had tried to stave off the evil day by previously writing cheques that had not been honoured.

'So either you don't have a bank account or your creditors know your cheques are worthless.' Oh, aren't we the Smarty Pants! 'Where did you get this two thousand?' he wanted to know.

'It's nothing to do with you!' she snapped, part of her wondering why she was still sitting there. Had that hard pavement addled her brain? Had the shock caused her to move in slow motion? Anyone would think she was enjoying having a slanging match with him.

'Since it looks a certainty that I'm going to be two thousand pounds out of pocket, I'd say it has everything to do with me!' he answered crisply.

Merren stared at him, totally perplexed. '*You're* going to be two thousand pounds out of pocket?'

He clearly had no belief in her puzzlement, but astonished her when he replied mockingly, 'I just know it's going to cost me that much to keep my word to my brother that I'd look after you.'

'You're suggesting you'd lend me the money?' she questioned, more to check that she'd got it right, that her brain wasn't so addled she was beginning to believe.

'I'm stating, not suggesting,' he began, but, waking up fast, Merren was butting in.

'Why should you?' she asked, starting to realise she must have landed in either a most generous or most crackpot family.

'Why wouldn't I?' he questioned back, his steady grey glance on her improved colour. 'Piers, whom I promise you has cost me more than forty pounds a week just lately with his lost causes, is about to leave the country to work abroad for a year. I think I'll be getting off lightly by making a final two-thousand-pound contribution to his waifs and strays fund.'

Insults she didn't need. Merren got to her feet, glad to find her legs were steady and that her dizzy spell was a thing of the past. 'Thank you for your hospitality,' she told him proudly, and, taking a few steps away from him, 'As for your money, I wouldn't dream of touching a penny of it.'

Grey eyes locked with deeply blue eyes. 'Fine,' he said, and, his glance flicking over her, 'You won't want to go through the streets looking like that.' And then, a decision made, 'I'll drive you home.'

Had she any other choice, Merren would have taken it. But, aside from the fact she knew she looked a wreck, she didn't so much as have the price of a twopenny bus ticket—if there was such a thing—and she certainly wasn't going to borrow from him. 'I live in Surrey,' she stated.

He didn't bat an eyelid, but escorted her out to where his beautiful-looking black Jaguar was parked.

They were silent for most of the drive. What was there to say? She didn't want to talk to him—she certainly had no intention of answering any of his questions—and he, likewise, didn't seem to want to talk to her.

In any case, she had a lot on her mind. Robert would be in despair when she told him she'd had the money but had lost it. She tried to think what else she could sell. There was her car, which was in good working order, but it was so old she'd be lucky if they got five hundred for it. Besides which, they seemed to need that car. In the six weeks since Robert and his family had moved in there had been countless visits *en masse* to the supermarket, and she'd taken her nieces, eight-year-old Queenie and six-year-old Kitty, out several times when Carol had been particularly edgy with them.

Merren wished her father would reply to Robert's letter. She knew her father didn't have a lot in the bank, but occasionally in the past, when her mother had hit hard times, she'd overcome her pride and accepted money he'd sent to tide them over.

Merren was just deciding that she would write to her father herself that night, when the man Jarad pulled up outside the detached house her father owned.

Jarad turned to her. 'You're looking better.'

'I'm a good actress,' she returned airily.

'So, I may have been wrong, and you may have been mugged.'

'Don't strain yourself!' she tossed at him, but belatedly remembering her manners, added politely, 'Thank you very much for bringing me home.'

'I'll bet that hurt!' Merren made to get out of the car. 'Will there be someone in to look after you? You're probably still in shock.'

She was more likely to have to look after them than they look after her. 'I live with my family,' she replied, and again made to get out of the car, when he stopped her.

He took out his wallet and extracted a business card. 'If you change your mind about the money—give me a ring.'

She took the card from him, but, knowing she wouldn't be phoning him, she didn't so much as look at it. 'Goodbye,' she said. His car was purring away before she was halfway up the garden path.

Ignoring the general clutter of family life when she went in, Merren picked up a note from the kitchen table. 'Gone to supermarket,' she read. Heartily glad that she had the chance to make herself more presentable before her brother and his family arrived home, Merren had a quick shower and changed into a cotton frock. The weather was sunny—she wished she felt the same.

She mourned the loss of her mother's ring—it had been so difficult to part with, and she felt quite dreadful that she had. Despite all her trials and tribulations her mother had always hung on to the ring, and had kept it safe for Merren, telling her that one day it would be hers.

And what had Merren done? Not only had she sold it but she'd lost the money she had received for it. Merren

just didn't know how she was going to face her brother
and confess what had happened.

Knowing she should go downstairs and try to restore
some order into the chaos of school bags, odd plimsolls,
socks and a half-eaten sandwich she'd seen lying about,
for once Merren squashed down her tidy soul and instead
got out her writing pad. It was an age since she had last
written to her father, and, much though she disliked asking him for money, she just didn't know what else she
could do. And he *was* family.

Having penned a very difficult letter—which had
started along the lines of 'as you know, Robert and his
family have, in straitened circumstances, come to live
with me here in your house'—she had gone on to tell
him of his lovely grandchildren, which she thought might
interest him, and ended with the crunch line, which had
been the most difficult of all to pen—if he could see his
way clear to send something to help pay off some outstanding bills. She signed her letter 'With love, Merren',
and went downstairs to tidy the cluttered sitting room and
kitchen.

Most probably they had all eaten dinner, but in case
they hadn't she began to peel a large panful of potatoes.
If they had eaten, the potatoes would do for tomorrow.
Now what was she going to tell Robert?

Merren knew she could only tell him the truth, but she
was feeling all stewed up inside about having to confess
when she heard her car on the drive.

She looked up as first her two nieces charged in.
'Hello, Aunty Merren.' They raced each other to the
bathroom, followed by her depressed-looking sister-in-
law, who was carrying a grizzling seven-month-old
Samuel. Robert, laden with shopping, followed on
behind.

'Shall I have the baby?' Merren asked, drying her hands and, while wanting to have what she had to tell her brother said and done with, found she also wanted to delay that dreadful moment when the expectant look on his face would die.

'He needs changing,' Carol answered, finding a smile, and disappeared to leave her alone with Robert.

'How did your job interview go?' Merren asked. Oh, how could she tell him?

'I didn't get it,' he said glumly, and, dropping the shopping down on the kitchen table, 'How about you— did you get it?'

He meant the money, she knew. 'N-no, actually, I...'

'Merren!' he exclaimed hoarsely. 'You couldn't sell Mother's ring? Oh Lord, this is the end!' He collapsed on to a kitchen chair, his head in his hands, his despair total. 'That's it— I'll go to prison, Carol will divorce me, I...'

'Robert!' Merren cried. Prison! This was the first she'd heard of the mention of prison! 'You're just being dramatic.'

'You don't know the half of it!'

'You've been in trouble before? Financial trouble?'

'You try bringing up a family—and maintaining a wife with expensive tastes,' he said bitterly.

As she looked at him, Merren saw for the first time that her big, dependable brother didn't seem so big and dependable after all. For the first time she noticed a certain weakness around his mouth. But that didn't make her love him less. He had their father's mouth. In fact he suddenly seemed a lot more like her father than her warm, generous-hearted mother.

'You have a lovely wife and a lovely family,' Merren

reminded him, not liking at all that he seemed to be taking a snipe at his wife.

'And I'll have the not so lovely bailiffs hammering on the door if those outstanding bills aren't settled by Monday,' he retorted sullenly. 'Are you sure you haven't got that money, Merren? You promised you'd sell that ring; you know you did.'

'I did sell it,' she confessed, but before she could tell him how the money had been stolen from her, his face was lit by a tremendous look of relief.

'You little terror!' he exclaimed, his face all huge smiles suddenly. 'You've been winding me up, Merren Shepherd! How much did you get for it?'

'T-two thousand, but...'

'Two thousand. Great!' He beamed. 'You were robbed, of course,' he said of the jeweller, Merren winced at the accuracy of the remark. 'But two thousand, as you know, will settle the blighters. Oh, Merren, it feels as if a ton of weight has been lifted off my shoulders. For a while there, you wicked imp, I felt quite suicidal.' Oh, heavens. Merren quailed at the enormity of what he had just confessed. 'Where is it?' he asked.

Good question. She felt tears prick the backs of her eyes. She turned away from him, knowing that, suicidal or not, she was going to have to douse that look of tremendous relief. 'I w-was...' she began, and half turned. It was a mistake to look at him. She loved him; he was her family. 'I'm—er—getting it tomorrow,' she heard herself state.

And Robert opined, 'Honestly, you'd think a jeweller of all people would have two thousand in cash on the premises, wouldn't you?'

'You would,' she agreed, and found she was taking up Robert's notion that she was going to have to go back to the jeweller's tomorrow because they normally paid via cheque and didn't deal much in cash. 'It's a security thing apparently.'

The conversation came to an end then, when Queenie and Kitty raced down the stairs and into the kitchen chorusing, 'I'm starving.'

Robert looked at Merren, who would normally have seen to their appetites, but she was reeling under the enormity of what she had done—and what she was panickingly realising she was going to have to do now.

'I've a letter I need to post,' she excused, and, finding a stamp in the bureau, went upstairs to collect the letter she had written to her father.

She stayed in her room some minutes, contemplating her options while the words 'prison', 'suicide', 'divorce', 'family break-up' whirled around in her head. She couldn't allow any of that to happen. So what options were there?

She'd post her letter to her father, though since he hadn't even bothered to reply to Robert's letter, she saw little hope that any plea from her would fare any better.

As if trying to avoid thinking of the man whose parting words had been, 'If you change your mind about the money—give me a ring,' she dwelt on the eldest member of their family, Uncle Amos.

Amos Yardley lived a ten-minute drive away, was her mother's brother, and Merren thought the world of him. He had been more of a father to her than her own, even before her parents had separated.

Dear Uncle Amos. 'Are you all right for money?' he'd asked when her mother had died. Merren had determined he would never know how the funeral had nearly cleaned her out; only the best had done for her mother.

'Absolutely!' she'd assured him. His two up and two

down cottage was collapsing about his ears—he was poorer than they were.

It was partly because she hadn't wanted him to worry, when she knew he could do nothing to help, that she hadn't told him the true reason Robert and his family had moved in with her. She had let Uncle Amos believe it was because it was so quiet and empty with her mother gone that she had asked Robert to move back to the family home.

But Uncle Amos, who was an inventor and often quite vague about matters outside his work, had given her a shrewd kind of look, as if suspecting she was doing a little inventing herself. To her mind, though, hers was a necessary invention. For, while Uncle Amos's inventions earned him nothing—he seemed to subsist by writing articles for clever magazines and barely scraped a living for himself—so Merren knew she would not be approaching him to help Robert out.

Which left her with the one option she was trying to avoid. She flicked her glance to the dressing table where, without so much as bothering to read it, she had dropped the man Jarad's card. A sick feeling entered her stomach. She didn't want to do it; she didn't.

Merren went over to the dressing table and picked up the card, and read it, and, oh, grief! She worked for an electronics company herself—only a tiny one by comparison, but large enough for her to be familiar with the name Roxford Waring, one of the biggest and most highly respected multinationals in the electronics field. The man Jarad had given her his personal business card, which also listed his home number. Oh, heaven's above, Jarad Montgomery was a director of Roxford Waring! Was she really contemplating contacting one of their board members with a view to borrowing some money from him?

Merren needed to think, so she escaped from the house and posted her letter, and, knowing the utter futility of it anyway, called in at the police station and reported having been mugged. She thought it unlikely they would catch the criminals, and knew she would never see her bag again.

Which, as she bowed to the inevitable and searched for a telephone kiosk—no way could she make this call from home—reminded her that she didn't even have the price of a phone call with her.

She didn't want to make that call; she didn't, she didn't. What she wanted to do was to go home, go to bed, and stick her head under the bedclothes—and stay there.

But there wasn't only herself to think of here. By reminding herself she had a deeply stressed brother, a deeply depressed sister-in-law, two young nieces and a baby nephew, Merren located a phone box.

She went in, grabbed at what courage she could find, quickly dialled the operator and asked the operator for a transfer charge call. And, even while she knew her name wouldn't mean a thing to Jarad Montgomery, she gave it to the operator—and waited.

The operator went off the line and Merren, feeling all hot and wishing she wasn't doing this, started to feel certain that even if Jarad Montgomery didn't refuse to accept the call from her, he most definitely wouldn't be expecting her to take him up on his offer of, 'If you change your mind about the money.'

By the time she heard his 'Hello' on the line, Merren was battling with pride—she didn't want his money anyway.

But—she needed it, so it was stiltedly that she answered, 'Hello, Ja... Mr Montgomery. Er—Merren Shepherd here.' Oh, drat, the operator would have already told him who his caller was.

'Merren Shepherd?' he replied, obviously not knowing her from Eve, for all he had accepted the charge. Either that, or he was playing with her.

That thought nettled her. 'As in "waif and stray",' she enlightened him shortly.

There was a pause, for all the world as if he was trying to place her. Then, 'That Merren Shepherd!' he responded smoothly, and Merren hated him again, with a vengeance.

But he was waiting, and there just wasn't any way of dressing it up. 'You were—um— Were you serious—about the m-money?' she questioned.

'Two thousand, you said.'

'Yes.'

'Come to my office tomorrow,' he instructed.

Her hands were all clammy; she gripped the phone hard. She swallowed. 'What time?'

'Eleven,' he said, and knowing she was going to have to take time off work, Merren also knew she was in no position to argue. Not that it would do her much good anyway—the line had gone dead.

Merren reeled out of the telephone kiosk, feeling a mixture of very intense emotions. She didn't like what she was doing, but by the sound of it Jarad Montgomery was prepared to help her.

She didn't like him, was niggled by his 'That Merren Shepherd!' as much as she was niggled by, 'Come to my office tomorrow' and his short 'Eleven' before he'd hung up.

No, she very definitely didn't like Mr Jarad Montgomery. But beggars couldn't be choosers, and Mr Jarad Montgomery was the only hope she'd got.

CHAPTER TWO

MERREN had a nightmare that night. She awoke frightened, breathless and crying out. Feeling stiff and bruised, she switched on the light and calmed herself by reflecting that it wasn't surprising she should dream violently of being hit, being chased—chased to the edge of a cliff— and of falling, falling.

She didn't know how long she had been yelling, but supposed it couldn't have been for very long, or very loudly either, because she hadn't disturbed anyone. Though, since she had moved up to the attic bedroom, it was unlikely anyone had heard her. No one was rushing up to rescue her from her night-time villains anyhow.

She felt wide awake, and would have liked to go down to the kitchen and make a warm drink, but feared, albeit that Robert and his family were heavy sleepers, that she might wake the baby. Baby Samuel had been fretful from birth, and, as she well knew, could cry for hours!

Not unnaturally, she supposed, thoughts of Jarad Montgomery came into her head. Had she really asked him for two thousand pounds? Had he really agreed to loan the money to her? And, if he had, how on earth was she going to pay it back?

That one thought kept her sleepless for the next hour. She still hadn't come up with any answer when from utter weariness, she fell asleep again. It was daylight the next time she awakened—and the baby was crying.

Merren left her bed to go down a flight of stairs to see to her little nephew. She couldn't remember having been hit on her shoulders, but her shoulders ached when she moved, while other parts of her body were vying with each other for rainbow effect bruising. The baby seemed heavier to lift out of his cot than usual, but, for once, he was being a little gentleman and decided to beam gummily at her after she'd changed him and given him a drink.

'You're a rascal,' she told him affectionately, and he grinned some more.

Then her dressing gowned brother came to join them, and, clearly wanting a word before anyone else was about, began, 'I've been thinking, Merren, that if I met you at the jeweller's at lunchtime, I could take the money and settle the...'

'Actually,' she butted in quickly, 'I'm—er—taking the day off work. I'll have the money back here by one.' Fingers crossed.

'Can I have the car?' he asked, assured of the money, wasting no time going on to his next priority.

But for once—feeling extremely vulnerable about money-carrying after her mugging yesterday—Merren just had to refuse.

'It's yours after one o'clock,' she replied, and would not be persuaded otherwise.

Once she'd handed the baby over, Merren bathed and returned to her room, and kept out of the way until Robert walked Queenie and Kitty to school and Carol was occupied with Samuel.

Merren studied her wardrobe. She did not want to remember the sketch she must have looked yesterday. She wouldn't forget Jarad Montgomery's, 'You won't want to go through the streets looking like that' in a hurry. Today, when she saw him again, she wanted to look smart. Why she should feel that way she didn't know. Her old friend pride, she supposed.

Dressed in her newest suit of deep blue, which brought out yet more blue to the colour of her eyes, Merren was walking through the revolving doors of the office of Roxford Waring before it so much as occurred to her that she might not even see Jarad Montgomery! 'Come to my office', he said. But he hadn't actually said he'd see her.

She approached the reception desk and almost asked if Mr Montgomery had left a package for her to collect. But quickly she pulled herself together. Get a grip! He'd want to know how she was going to pay him back—if only *she* knew! No one was going to hand over that sort of money to a complete stranger without asking some pretty pertinent questions.

'I'm here to see Mr Jarad Montgomery.' She smiled at the smart receptionist. 'Merren Shepherd,' she gave her name.

She was expected! Merren rode up in the lift with her insides all of a churn. She did so hope she wasn't here on a fool's errand. He'd meant it, hadn't he? She just wouldn't be able to go home again, wouldn't be able to face Robert if he hadn't.

She tapped on the door she had been directed to. She'd expected his PA to invite her in. But the door was opened by Jarad Montgomery himself. Though for a moment he did not invite her in, but just stood there looking at her. But, while his glance went over her blonde-streaked reddish hair—tidy today in comparison to yesterday, for all she still wore it loose—Merren took a moment to study him.

He was as tall as she remembered. But in his immaculate business suit, crisp shirt and tie, he looked even more authoritative today than he had yesterday—and that was saying something.

'You've polished up well,' he drawled, and suddenly her nerves were disappearing.

You're looking pretty snappy yourself. 'I made an effort,' she countered, hoping he would think she was joking.

'Come in.'

Merren entered his office, noticed the communicating door to his PA's office was closed, and was glad about that. By the look of it he was treating this as a private matter.

'How are you feeling?' he enquired, indicating a chair before going and taking a seat behind his desk. 'You were pretty shaken up yesterday,' he recalled.

'The bruises will soon fade,' she smiled. And, not wanting to prolong this interview any longer than she had to, she went on, 'I'm sorry I had to reverse the charges last night when I rang. I didn't have any change with me.'

'You didn't want to ring from your home?'

Sharp! Merren quickly realised they didn't come very much sharper than him. 'I—er—didn't—don't want my family to know that I was mugged.'

'Or that you were robbed of that two thousand pounds you were carrying?' She didn't answer. 'Where did you get it?' he wanted to know.

'I came by it honestly,' she bristled—but, recognising that perhaps he had some right to know, she added more evenly, 'I sold an item of jewellery.'

'It was yours to sell?' he asked quickly.

She resented his question, and resented his tone. 'I...' she began sharply back, and then realised she couldn't afford to fire up at him. She needed his help. And, she supposed reluctantly, his question, since he didn't know the first thing about her, was a fair one. 'It was a ring belonging to my mother.'

'Your mother's in need of two thousand pounds?'

'My mother died ten months ago,' she replied stonily.

'So the money's for you. What for?' He pursued his line of questioning, and, as if he'd summed up why she hadn't wanted her family to know, his look was suddenly fierce. 'You're pregnant!' he rapped.

'No, I'm not!' she snapped back. Honestly! 'Chance would be a fine thing!' His hint about what she wanted the money for infuriated her!

'You haven't...?'

'I don't.'

'Not ever?' he questioned, his anger gone, polite interest taking its place.

'I'm working on it!' she retorted crisply. Was she really having this discussion? 'I told you—I needed that money to pay some bills.' She brought the subject back to where she wanted it. She took a steadying breath, her pride buckling as she made herself ask, 'Do you have the m-money for me?'

His answer was to open a desk drawer and withdraw a plain envelope. He stretched over and placed the envelope on the corner of his desk nearest to her. 'Cash,' he stated, seeming to know she wasn't interested in a cheque.

'Thank you,' she said, not touching the envelope. 'Do you want me to sign something to say I've received it?'

'Not necessary,' he replied.

'Oh,' she murmured. 'Er—about paying it back.'

Jarad Montgomery stared at her, seemed about to say something, but instead invited, 'Go on.'

'Well—I—that is, I think you've already worked out,

as I did last night, that it—um—may be some while before I'll be in a position to repay you.'

'I appreciate your honesty,' he drawled. 'Though I can't quite remember asking you for repayment.'

'You can't be lending—giving—me the money out of the goodness of your heart!' she erupted.

'You're suggesting I have a black heart?' he enquired coolly.

She wasn't. How could she think that when he was doing this enormous deed for her? But, 'You must want something in return?' she said in a rush as the thought came. She knew she was green, but nobody parted with that sort of money for nothing.

Jarad stared at her for long, silent moments. Silkily then, he murmured, 'You're prepared to sell your—um—services?'

She had the most awful pride-denting feeling that he was playing with her, and—even while ready to accept his enormous favour—Merren felt she hated him. 'I'm a very good secretary,' she informed him bluntly.

'You have a job?' He seemed surprised.

'I rang my employer this morning and asked for the day off, out of my holiday entitlement,' she answered stiffly. 'I could work evenings and weekends if you've any secretarial...'

'I've a perfectly efficient PA.' He turned down her offer.

And Merren was out of ideas. 'You've a perfectly efficient domestic staff too,' she thought out loud, remembering his well cared for, polished and gleaming house.

'You'd do cleaning?' He stared at her as if she was some new kind of species as yet unknown to him.

'I'm prepared to do anything legal.'

'I see,' he murmured, and, every bit as if it needed

some thinking about, he continued, 'You'd better come and see me tomorrow—I'll let you know my requirements then. Er—don't bring an apron.' Merren was off her chair making for the door when his voice stopped her. 'Haven't you forgotten something?' She spun round, and inwardly groaned—she had forgotten to pick up the money.

It was him! Somehow he had the power to unsettle her, making her swing from an urgent desire to hit him, to wanting to smile and be grateful. She went back to the desk and picked up the envelope. 'Thank you,' she said quietly, with what dignity she could find.

'Stay put,' was her answer. 'You're obviously not safe to be let out on your own; I'll get a driver to take you home.'

The sauce of it! It gave her a great deal of pleasure to be able to tell him, 'Actually, I have my car today.'

Her pleasure was short-lived. 'I'll get someone from Security to walk you to it,' he pronounced.

Merren couldn't remember actually saying goodbye to him, but as she and the security guard left the Roxford Waring building she owned to feeling glad to have the solidly built fit-looking man by her side. That episode yesterday had left her feeling more vulnerable than she'd realised. Not that she thanked Jarad Montgomery for his thoughtfulness. Him and his 'not safe to be let out on your own'! Huh!

The closer she drove to her home, however, Merren began to experience a decided aversion to handing Jarad Montgomery's money over to her brother. The feeling was ridiculous; she knew it was. For goodness' sake, the whole point of her visit to the Roxford Waring building had been to get the money for Robert. Her reluctance, she suddenly comprehended, was because once the money was gone from her keeping, gone to pay Robert's long outstanding bills, she would be committed. Committed—in debt to Jarad Montgomery.

Robert came hurrying out of the house the moment he saw her car, and, seeing his tense expression, Merren could not hesitate to hand him the money. 'I won't forget this,' he beamed, but she guessed, as she handed over her car keys too, that forget it he would.

She went indoors; Carol was out somewhere with the baby—and the house was a tip. Merren went and changed out of her suit. Dressed in cotton trousers and a tee shirt, she was vacuuming the sitting room carpet when thoughts of Jarad Montgomery returned to disturb her.

She supposed, in view of what had happened, it wasn't surprising he should be in her head so frequently. He had just done her one very generous kindness. That she was going to have to pay for that kindness by some means or other was only to be expected. Besides, she wouldn't have it any other way. Pride alone decreed that.

'Come and see me tomorrow,' he'd said. He hadn't said where, he hadn't said when, but, since tomorrow was Saturday, he must mean that she should call at his home to discover in what way he'd decided she should repay him.

Having cleaned and tidied everywhere, while knowing it would be utter chaos again within hours of her family coming home, Merren made a cake to take to Uncle Amos the next day. Her mother had always presented him with a cake every Saturday. It had pleased Merren to take that small pleasure over. Uncle Amos was very partial to sultana cake.

Bertie Armstrong rang around seven that evening. He and Merren were around the same age, and had always been the best of friends. 'I'm going to The Bull for a jar later on—fancy coming?' he asked.

Merren wasn't particularly keen, but, having told Jarad Montgomery that she could work evenings and weekends, decided to take Bertie up on his offer. Heaven alone knew when, after she saw the man Jarad tomorrow, she would have another evening free for a 'jar'.

'Nineish?' she enquired.

'I'll call for you,' he said, and, even though she would be seeing him later, such was their friendship that they stayed chatting about inconsequential matters for the next twenty minutes. But, good friend though Bertie was, she couldn't tell him of the recent happenings in her life.

Having gone to The Bull with Bertie for a drink, Merren returned home just after eleven to find the house in darkness, everyone in bed. She had thought her few hours in the uncomplicated company of Bertie Armstrong had relaxed her. But later she had a frightening nightmare similar to the one she'd had the night before, and she began to realise that the trauma of being the victim of a street assault, didn't end once you'd picked yourself up and dusted yourself down.

Eventually she managed to get back to sleep, but was awakened early by the baby testing his lung power. It amazed her that she could hear him when no one else could. Though, since his mother coped with his incessant demands on a daily basis, Merren felt Carol could be forgiven for pulling the bedclothes over her head and hoping someone else would attend to him. Merren got out of bed.

She was uncertain about what time she should go and see Jarad Montgomery, but as it was her habit to go and spend some time with Uncle Amos on a Saturday morning, she decided to leave her visit to Jarad Montgomery until the afternoon. He knew where she lived, she was in the phone book, and if he got tired of waiting she felt confident he would telephone and leave some short, and to the point message.

Realising that nerves were getting to her at the prospect of seeing Jarad again, and that she was getting uptight and just a little irked by him—though how she could when she owed him so much—not least her brother's peace of mind and his family's security—Merren took herself off to see her Uncle Amos.

'Had a good week?' she asked him as she replenished his cake tin.

'Running into trouble with my latest brainwave,' he acknowledged. 'How about you?'

No way could she tell the dear man about the horror of Thursday, or her visit to see Jarad Montgomery yesterday. Uncle Amos would be up in arms that anyone had dared to assault her, and he would fret himself silly that he wasn't able to help with the money.

'Fine,' she smiled. 'Shall I make some coffee?'

'Er—the kitchen's in a bit of a state.'

She'd never known it any different. After coffee, and as her mother had before her, Merren returned to the kitchen and got busy with his backlog of used crockery. 'Fancy coming to lunch with us tomorrow?' she invited, knowing in advance that he wouldn't.

'After last time?' he grinned, and Merren grinned back. Uncle Amos had been married once, before—as he'd told Merren—his wife had got fed up with him and had gone off. There had been no children from the marriage; his only dealings had been with Merren and her brother, who'd been vastly different from the screeching and over-excited Queenie and Kitty, who'd shattered his eardrums that Sunday lunchtime when, against his better judgement, he'd decided to take a look at his great-nieces and great-nephew. Baby Samuel's lung power that day had been astronomical. 'Are they any better behaved?' he wanted to know.

'The girls are—er—settling in their new school,' Merren answered diplomatically.

She felt in much better spirits when she left than she had when she'd arrived. But anxiety started to nibble away at her as she drove back to her home. There was no putting it off. She was going to have to go and see Jarad Montgomery that afternoon.

With that visit in mind, and again finding her confidence in need of a boost, Merren changed into a smart cream linen skirt and jacket, checked what little make-up she wore was just right, also checked that she didn't have a hair out of place, and, by using avoidance tactics, managed to get out of the house untouched by small, but inquisitive jammy fingers.

She parked near to where Jarad Montgomery lived, but owned to feeling on edge when walking to his house, she had to pass the spot where she had been set upon two days ago. Telling herself not to be silly, she was nevertheless glad to make it to Jarad Montgomery's front door. She rang the bell, and waited.

Jarad Montgomery himself opened the door, though why her heart should pick up a beat when she saw him, she had no idea. Probably because he looked a shade surprised to see her there. Had he forgotten she was going to call today?

She thought she should remind him. 'You said I should come and see you today,' she began quietly, when all of a sudden she saw that two women, both carrying hand-bags, and clearly on their way out, were coming along the hall behind him. One of the women was touching sixty, the other was somewhere in her early thirties, Merren judged. Both were smartly and expensively dressed. 'I've called at an inconvenient time,' Merren began to apologise as the two ladies halted at his shoulder.

'Not at all,' Jarad was beginning smoothly, when he glanced from her to the two females who were positively beaming at him. He paused for the briefest of moments, then, glancing back to Merren, he was suddenly all smiles himself as he stated, 'This is a delightful surprise,' and, while she stared at him—*delightful?*—he was going on, 'I hadn't expected to see you before this evening.'

He'd thought she would call that evening to discuss the money she owed him? Well, she didn't want to discuss it in front of these other people, that was for sure. Merren took a tiny step back, but before she could tell him that she would call later, that perhaps she should have telephoned first, he had taken a swift hold of her upper arm and was drawing her closer to his front door.

'Don't be shy.' He was smiling. *Shy?* 'My mother and sister are just leaving, but come and say hello to them before they go.' And before Merren could do more than think his manners were truly outstanding, she found herself in the hall with him, the front door closed, as he made the introductions.

'I'm so pleased to see you, Merren,' his mother beamed; her manners, Merren swiftly realised, every bit as outstanding as her son's.

'Do you live in London?' his sister, Veda Partridge, smilingly wanted to know.

'Surrey.'

'Do you and Jarad often get to meet?' Mrs Montgomery enquired pleasantly.

'Mother!' Jarad inserted warningly. 'We saw each other yesterday, and the day before that, but I wouldn't have told you anything about Merren had I thought you'd give her the third degree.' And while Merren went a pretty pink, because Jarad had obviously told his mother and sister that he'd loaned her some money, his mother suddenly seemed overjoyed by what he had just said.

'Oh, I'm so sorry,' Mrs Montgomery apologised earnestly. 'I've made you blush,' she added, and, to Merren's amazement, she kissed her cheek and said hurriedly, 'We're going before I embarrass you further.'

'Bye, Merren,' Veda smiled.

'You must come down to Hillmount as soon as you can,' his mother invited, and while Merren stood there— it didn't seem to her to be very polite to suggest that the Montgomery family were a touch on the strange side— mother and daughter bade Jarad goodbye and went cheerfully from his home.

Jarad closed the door after them and guided Merren into the drawing room she had barely taken in last Thursday. It was high-ceilinged, elegant, with several extremely good oil paintings adorning the walls, and yet was a comfortable room with its well-padded sofas and scattering of chairs and low tables.

'I'm sorry about that,' he said, as he invited her to take a seat.

She opted for one of the easy chairs, and he did the same. 'I know I'm in no position to mind, but I'd have preferred it had you not told your family about the money,' Merren responded, to what she thought was his apology for discussing the matter with his mother and sister.

She was therefore a little shaken when he denied that he had done any such thing. 'Anything to do with that money is just between you and me,' he asserted evenly.

Merren stared at him. 'You didn't mention it in any

way?' Looking steadily at her, he shook his head. She owned she was puzzled. 'Then—what was that "I wouldn't have told you anything about Merren" about? You must have told them something about...' Her voice trailed off. 'Were you meaning you told them about me being mugged? Though that doesn't...'

'That doesn't explain why my mother and sister would be ready to give you the third degree,' he took over. 'I'm afraid, Merren,' he went on pleasantly, 'that your timing today could have been better. Though I must say your blush was right on cue.'

'Is everybody in your family eccentric?' she enquired nicely, the fog getting thicker instead of clearing.

'My father, bless his heart, keeps strictly out of it. I wish,' he muttered, 'that I were allowed to do the same.'

'You mentioned explaining.'

'I'm not doing a very good job, am I?' He looked at her, smiled at her—it was rather a nice smile she thought—and she waited. 'So here goes,' Jarad continued, and went on, 'For years now my mother—my sister holds the same view—has been of the opinion that I should marry and settle down.'

'You're not married?' Merren queried, feeling oddly content that it should be so. Weird—that mugging Thursday had a lot to answer for.

'Never felt the need,' he replied. 'To be frank, I very much enjoy my life just as it is.'

'You don't feel at all that you're missing anything?' He didn't answer, but thinking about it, his home, his position on the board of Roxford Waring, and glancing at him—a good-looking, all virile male—there was no need for him to answer—he had it all. 'That was a dumb question,' she granted. 'Your mother doesn't know your views about...'

'Oh, she knows. I've repeatedly told her. But that's never stopped her from doing a trawl of her friends every now and then for likely daughters, nieces, friends of daughters, friends of nieces—it's been hell!'

Shame. 'There must have been one or two acceptable ones.'

'Acceptable for what? If I'd given in and taken just one of them out, my mother would have been wondering what to give us for an engagement present!'

'As bad as that?'

'Believe it. Though,' he conceded, 'things did get a little better when Piers left university and came here to live with me.'

'Your mother thought it better that you looked after him?'

'That too, of course. But mainly she saw that if she was wasting her time with me, then Piers was just coming up to marriageable age. Piers is fifteen years younger than me. Love my mother though I do, I loved her more when she started to leave me alone and give Piers the treatment. Though in his case it was granddaughters of friends and great-nieces who were brought out for inspection.'

'Is that why your brother took off abroad?' Merren asked. It seemed logical. 'To get away?'

'No, nothing like that. Piers had a whale of a time. He thoroughly enjoyed not having to hunt, but finding his supper there, handed to him on a plate.' Which wouldn't suit you, Jarad Montgomery, Merren guessed. He'd want to hunt. He wouldn't want conquests handed to him on a plate. Which was why, she saw, he'd been unable to find a flicker of interest for any of the women his mother had introduced. 'Piers came out of it unscathed, and has gone abroad for a year because that's what he always planned to do. Which, Merren Shepherd,' Jarad said,

'brings me round to letting you know why I've been con-
fiding what is exclusively a family matter.'

Merren looked at him warily. He was serious now,
unsmiling. Why, she wondered, when she felt certain he
was a rather private man, with a great affection for his
family, *would* he tell her, a person he barely knew, details
about his family—as he just had?

'It's got something to do with the money, hasn't it?'
was the best guess she could come up with. 'The two
thousand pounds you're out of pocket?'

'Got it in one,' Jarad congratulated her. 'When earlier
I opened my door and my mother and Veda walked in,
I feared the worst. Piers only left last Thursday, and al-
ready I'm back being the target!'

'You think they'll revert back to trying to get you to
the altar?'

'I know it!' he stated unequivocally. 'They've started
already. My mother, ably abetted by Veda, came today
to insist I'd be letting her down if I didn't pay Hillmount
a visit next weekend. They're up to something.'

'You think they'll have someone on hand for you to—
er—partner?'

'I'd bank on it. I told them I'd got plans—and of
course they wanted to know what plans.'

'Well, if you've something on, surely they won't expect...'

'I've nothing on that's so important I can't change it.
But, having had a breathing space while Piers was here,
I saw at once that the year ahead was going to be pretty
diabolical if I couldn't head them off.' He broke off for
a moment, but then resumed, 'Which was why, partly for
the hell of it, partly in an attempt to knock on the head
any "casual" introductions they have lined up for me in
the coming twelve months, I told them that I'd met some-

one special and that I didn't want to miss any chance of
seeing her. That I hoped they'd understand, and not be
hurt that I wouldn't be going down to Hampshire next
weekend.'

'You're seeing someone special?' Merren checked.

'I don't know anyone *that* special,' Jarad denied, with
a grin. 'But by that time both my mother and sister were
quite positive I was going steady.'

'Didn't they want to know more about her?'

'You're getting to know them,' he commented lightly.
'I told them they'd meet her in due time—which, left in
peace, would give me time to work out my next move.
Happy when at last it appeared I'd been nailed, they were
on the point of leaving, in fact were all at the bottom end
of the hall, when you rang the bell.'

Merren looked at him, but when he held her gaze it
seemed he had nothing more to say, and she played back
in her mind Jarad opening his door to her, his mother
and sister appearing behind him, their questions, Mrs
Montgomery kissing her cheek. Merren's eyes widened.

'They think—th-think I'm your steady girlfriend, don't
they?' she gasped. And, as more brain power arrived—'This is a delightful surprise,' he'd said!—
'That's what you wanted them to believe, wasn't it?'

'Not until I glanced at my mother and saw that eager
glad light in her eye. Both she and Veda were speculating
like mad— Is she the one? It seemed a shame then to
waste the opportunity—tailor-made—on my doorstep.'

'Opportunity?' Merren questioned, not certain how she
felt about any of this, but striving to keep up. 'You used
me to...'

'Don't look at it that way,' he cut in.

'What other way is there to look at it?' she bridled.
'In that one glance to your mother you read the situation

and decided to make capital out of it—using me! How else am I supposed to look at it?'

'Are you always this fiery?' he wanted to know, and, not giving her chance to answer, he went on, 'If you'll bear with me for a short while, I'm sure you'll agree that we can work everything out to our mutual advantage.'

Merren opened her mouth. Mutual advantage! He was hinting at the money she owed him—must be. Oh, crumbs—whatever was worked out she was still left owing him two thousand pounds—which she hadn't a hope of repaying. 'I'm listening,' she mumbled.

'It's obvious to me that you can't manage on your salary or you'd never have got yourself into debt.' Given that Robert and his family were in receipt of State benefits, a good part of her salary went to assist a family of five, but she wasn't about to tell him that. 'Which makes it equally obvious that you're never going to be in a position to repay the two thousand I handed you yesterday.' Merren shifted uncomfortably in her seat, deciding she could do without this tell-the-truth-and-shame-the-devil tactic. 'Equally obvious, too, is the fact that, while you might get yourself into debt, you have every intention of settling all those debts—which is why you're here now.'

'You said to come.'

'You needn't have.'

'You know where I live,' she thought to mention.

'You wouldn't have come otherwise?'

It didn't take any thinking about. 'Oh, I would,' she answered. Pride, honesty. She'd have come. 'It's a pig being honest.'

'Good,' Jared smiled, having no doubts about her honesty, apparently—she had an idea he would never have introduced her to his mother and sister the way he had if

he'd had any doubts about her. 'It's clearly important to
you that we find some way for you to pay back that
money—you wouldn't be here at all otherwise.'

'You've found some work for me?'

He smiled. 'I've found a job for you—if you're willing
to do it.'

'I've told you, I'm prepared to do anything legal.'

'Oh, this is legal,' he assured her. Then, evenly, he
enquired, 'How would you like to be my steady girlfriend
for a year?'

Merren stared at him. She wasn't sure that her jaw
didn't drop. 'You're not serious?'

'I promise you I am.'

'But—but—we don't even know each other!' she protested.

'We don't have to—it will be an in-name-only courtship.'

'For your mother's sake—er—or rather, yours?'

'Don't forget about my sister being my mother's trusty
lieutenant.'

Merren didn't like it. 'You'd deceive them, carry on
deceiving them? For a year?'

'Until Piers gets back and they can turn their attentions
on him.'

She still didn't like it. 'Can't you just explain that you
don't want their attention? That you're happy as you
are?'

'Do you think I haven't tried?'

'It didn't work?'

'Three weeks at most is the longest they've backed off.
You've a family yourself. You know the pressure that
sometimes brings.' Didn't she just! If it wasn't for Robert
and that two thousand pounds he needed she wouldn't be
in this mess. 'Friends, acquaintances, they understand the

word "No"; families just don't recognise it. Unfortunately, where you can tell friends or acquaintances where to go, if you're so minded, some family members—who take liberties friends wouldn't dream of entertaining—cannot be told.'

'But have to be shown?' Merren queried.

'Exactly.'

Merren still didn't like it any better. But she owed him. 'What would I have to do?' she asked reluctantly.

'Probably nothing at all,' Jarad answered. 'But if for the next twelve months you could be "on call", as it were, it should resolve matters to everyone's satisfaction.'

'By "on call" you mean, let you have my phone number, and be available to drive here the moment you ring—that sort of thing?'

'I doubt very much that I'll have to bother you,' Jarad commented easily. 'Though, with your permission, I'd like to drop your name into the conversation whenever I feel it appropriate. My mother seldom calls to see me—which is why today's visit has such ominous overtones. Ye gods, my brother only left the country a couple of days ago!'

'You—um—don't think you're being just a little unfair to your mother and sister—fooling them...?'

'Unfair! Was it fair of them to poke their matrimonially-minded noses in, and then to spoil what is a very enjoyable lifestyle?'

'Life's a toad!' she commiserated, though with not much sympathy. But seriously needed to recap. 'You're saying, Mr Montgomery, that all I have to do to repay that loan is to be ready to shoot over here to your home occasionally when the call comes?'

'The situation may never arise, as I've said. But that's about it.'

'Two thousand pounds seems a lot of money to pay for something that may never arise,' her innate honesty compelled her to point out.

Steady grey eyes pinned her deeply blue ones. 'Call it a retainer,' he suggested, and before she could comment on that, he added, 'Just in case, you'd better recite the name "Jarad" ten times a day.'

Merren laughed. She guessed it wouldn't look good were she to dash 'on call' to see him, to greet him as 'Mr Montgomery' in front of his mother. 'I'll practise,' she promised, and, unable to think of anything else they might need to discuss, she got to her feet.

Jarad went to the front door with her. But before he opened it he looked down at her as they stood there, and told her, 'I think you and I are going to fare very well together, Merren Shepherd.' Then he gave a sigh, 'Such a pity—I may never need to see you again.'

Merren laughed again. He seemed to have that effect on her—or was it just that she was relieved that she wasn't going to have to work every night and all weekends? 'We can only hope,' she grinned, and went home still smiling.

When she thought over all that had been said, as she did on that drive home, Merren realised that, when it came to it, even though it was pretty obvious that she'd have to drop everything and dash if his phone call came—a two-thousand-pound retainer wasn't half bad.

She pulled up at her home, fancying that she could see a glimmer of a silver lining behind her dark cloud.

CHAPTER THREE

SUNDAY passed with Merren unable to get Jarad Montgomery out of her head. Today it seemed incredible to her that all she had to do to earn the money he had so generously given her was to pretend, though only to his mother and sister, that she and Jarad were an 'item'.

All she had to do in order to earn that 'retainer', it seemed, was to respond to a telephone call—that, according to Jarad, might never come—and rush to his home. Merren owned that she wasn't very comfortable with the idea of having taken that money when most likely she would have to do absolutely nothing to earn it. On the other hand, she wasn't very comfortable either with the notion of deliberately taking part in the deception of his two female relatives if called upon to do so.

Having thought that, as the days progressed, the arrangement she had agreed with Jarad would sit more comfortably with her, she found herself mistaken. She woke up on Monday—and it didn't seem right. And on Tuesday she *knew* that it just wasn't right—and that nothing would make it right. Nothing would except paying him back that two thousand. It had nothing to do with pride—they had made a bargain. But she was getting the better part of the bargain—and she should never have agreed to it, should never have taken the money.

Merren couldn't think what else she could have done in the circumstances but have agreed to it—and have taken that money. But as she made her way home from her place of work that night—Robert had borrowed her car—she decided that as soon as her brother found himself a job and was no longer in need of her help she would start saving, and would pay Jarad Montgomery back every penny.

Perhaps it was pride after all, she mused as she turned into the avenue where she lived. In any event, it was important to her that she lost the 'waif and stray' label that Jarad had once stuck on her.

All thoughts of the man she had made that most unusual contract with went abruptly, though only temporarily, from her mind when, reaching the house, she saw a dilapidated old car standing on the drive.

Hoping against hope that Robert hadn't accumulated fresh debt by purchasing the piece of scrap metal, or, worse, that he hadn't done a part exchange deal, handing her car in for cash and that rusting heap, Merren hurried indoors and was relived on two fronts. The car wasn't a new acquisition of her brother's. It belonged to her father—her father had arrived.

'When did you get here?' she asked, after greeting him.

'About ten minutes ago. Carol was going to make me something to eat, but...'

Carol, a tired and worn-out-looking Carol had her hands full with yelling Samuel and peevish Queenie and Kitty, who 'didn't want to' whatever was suggested.

Merren automatically held out her arms for the baby. He still yelled, but at least Carol looked relieved to hand him over for a few minutes while she had a stern parental word with her daughters.

'Can you stay for a few days?' Merren asked her father, when the baby's cries had lessened a few decibels.

'I thought I might,' he replied, and Merren relinquished the attic bedroom, to which she had so recently moved. Still, the sitting room sofa was large, and at five foot eight, she was of slender build, and it would only be for a few days.

She heard her car on the drive, and when Robert came in, and had greeted their father, she handed the baby to her brother and set about making a meal for them all. She sorely wanted to ask her father if he'd received her letter, if he'd arrived in response to it. Oh, wouldn't it be wonderful if he'd come to help them out of the financial mess they were in?

Correction, the financial mess *she* was in. By now Robert was debt-free. But she would much prefer to owe her father two thousand than she would Jarad Montgomery.

Dinner was a noisy meal, most of it coming from the baby, who Carol said was teething. 'Does that kid never stop bawling?' Lewis Shepherd asked his daughter as he joined her at the kitchen sink.

Merren supposed that Samuel did—but wasn't surprised when her father said he was going out. What did surprise her was that he said he thought he'd go and see his brother-in-law, Amos. Uncle Amos and her father had always disliked each other intensely. Not to put too fine a point on it, Merren had only ever known them at daggers drawn with each other. 'Give Uncle Amos my love,' she smiled—perhaps the years had mellowed both of them.

Apparently not. Merren spent the time in her father's absence in changing her bed and making her room more masculine for her father, and also in doing a general tidy-up downstairs. Her father was scowling when he came in, and she guessed that there was still no love lost between the two men. Lewis Shepherd remembered his manners sufficiently to wish her, Carol and Robert goodnight, however, and then went straight to bed. Merren surmised that he must be exceedingly tired after his drive up that day from Cornwall.

Her assumption, however, that her father would stay with them for a few days, and that she would be sleeping on the sitting room sofa for only a few days, proved erroneous. A month later and her father, who she now knew had given up his job to come and see them, was showing no signs of returning to Cornwall. Nor was he making any contribution to the household expenses—and Merren's resources were creaking from the strain.

Since it was his house, and they were all living there rent-free, Merren didn't see how she could possibly ask him if he wouldn't mind chipping in for the odd box of cereal. But the silver lining she'd thought she'd seen on her dark cloud that Saturday five weeks ago, had most definitely tarnished at the edges. Robert had revealed how he'd mentioned to their father that the immediate financial crisis he'd asked his help with, was over. To which their father had apparently replied he was glad about that, because he was having a struggle making ends meet himself.

Merren drove back from taking Uncle Amos his Saturday sultana cake, resolving that she shouldn't feel down. So what if the house was overcrowded and what sleep she did get was invariably punctuated with nightmares? Uncle Amos was a love, and she was seeing Bertie Armstrong and a few of the others down at The Bull for a drink that night. So, okay, it wasn't life in the fast lane, but...

Suddenly, as she turned the car into the avenue, all thought ceased. There was a car parked outside her house. A Jaguar. She knew that car! Hadn't she once been a passenger in it?

Suddenly her heartbeat went into overdrive. Jarad Montgomery had said he would phone her if the need arose. Or—that was the arrangement she'd thought they'd made. And perhaps she'd grown a little bit complacent when a whole month had gone by and no call had come. Perhaps she had even started to think that his call would never come—hadn't she privately been thinking of trying to save, of trying to repay him the money? But, unless she was very much mistaken, Jarad Montgomery had decided to bypass the telephone system in favour of a personal visit.

She parked on the drive and hurried in, her glance taking in the general clutter of the sitting room and the two small girls who were trying to join in the conversation their mother was having with the tall black-haired man who was getting to his feet, while the baby grizzled on.

'Jarad!' Merren smiled, holding down her 'oh, crumbs' feelings. But, wanting none of her family to know anything of their financial arrangement, 'I didn't know you were coming over. You should have phoned,' she hinted.

'I should have,' he agreed smoothly.

'Have you been here long?'

'Ten minutes!' Queenie answered for him.

'How long's ten minute's, Mummy?' Kitty wanted to know.

'Would you like some tea?' Merren offered her guest politely.

'It's a splendid afternoon. Perhaps we could have it in the garden,' Jarad suggested.

'Yes!' whooped Queenie, when Merren was certain the children hadn't been invited.

'Yes!' Kitty echoed.

'I'll bring it out in a few minutes,' Merren hinted, and

as Jarad went out into the garden and Carol called Queenie and Kitty back, Merren went into the kitchen and made some tea.

When she would have placed more than two cups and saucers on the tray, however, her sister-in-law stopped her. 'I'll have mine in here, and so will the girls,' she added firmly, when they looked ready to sprint outside.

Merren was grateful to her, and for once she was deaf to all wailed protests as her nieces became more and more convinced that their aunt and her visitor were desperate for their company.

'Robert and Father out?' she asked as she picked up the tray.

'They've gone in your father's car for an early evening paper—it takes two of them to carry it, apparently,' Carol said, more waspishly than humorously.

Merren took the tray outside. By the sound of it her father and brother would be back at any moment. She hated deception, and wouldn't mind at all if Jarad had gone by the time they returned.

Jarad came forward and took the tray from her and carried it over to the garden furniture situated in the shade of a whitebeam tree. 'Er—I haven't told any of my family about our—er—um—arrangement,' Merren said in a rush as they each took their seats on either side of the table.

'Then I won't either,' he answered solemnly, and Merren just had to laugh—what was it about this man? One second she was feeling all strung up, and the next he was making her laugh. 'How was Uncle Amos?' he enquired conversationally, his grey eyes on the upward curve of her smiling mouth.

'He's as lively as ever,' she answered.

'But doesn't care for children?' he enquired as she handed him his tea.

'You guessed?'

'Apparently you take your uncle a cake every Saturday, but this Saturday, when your nieces wanted you to take them with you, you refused.'

Thank you, Queenie. 'I'm the original hard-hearted Hannah,' Merren accepted lightly.

Jarad's eyes met hers. 'That's not what I've been hearing,' he said quietly.

'You haven't been asking questions?' Merren erupted. Only to feel a fool a moment later when he surveyed her coolly. Why would he ask questions, for goodness' sake? She and her family were of no interest to him.

'I didn't have to ask anything,' he replied after some moments of just looking at her.

'Queenie?'

'Admirably assisted by Kitty,' he agreed. 'Your sister-in-law had to disappear for two minutes—something domestic in the baby department. I confess,' he continued with a flicker of a smile, 'that I'm more comfortable conversing with ladies around twenty years older than your niece. Anyhow, I made the effort and asked them how they liked school.'

'A fairly safe topic.'

'So I thought. I swear I wasn't prying when, in the space of the next two minutes, the two little ones filled me in on how they were going to a new school because Daddy doesn't work any more, and they came to live with you because you've got lots of rooms—only you haven't any more because Daddy's Daddy has moved in as well.' Jarad paused, and then, giving her a direct look, 'Do you really sleep on the sitting room sofa?'

Merren stared at him. He sounded a touch concerned.

She didn't want that. 'I wouldn't say I sleep a lot,' she smiled. And, when her smile didn't bring a responding smile, she continued, 'Anyhow, the house belongs to my father, so he'd every right to move back in.'

'When did he move out?'

Honestly! Merren looked at him exasperatedly. 'Well, if you must know, he and my mother separated when I was a toddler. But,' she went on quickly before he could ask anything else, 'you haven't come here to listen to any of that.'

Jarad neither said that he had or he hadn't. What he did do, was smile a smile that was suddenly stunningly loaded with charm. 'Are you free to have dinner with me tonight?' he asked.

For no reason her heart seemed to take a giddy leap. Grief, if he went around prefixing every invitation with a smile like that, Merren doubted that he ever had a refusal. She, who had decided she was made of sterner stuff, pulled herself together.

'The one night of the year when I already have a date, and you turn up!' she said disgustedly, but found another, answering smile.

He grinned—and her heart did that ridiculous flip again. 'Break it,' he urged.

Merren knew that all she had to do was to ring Bertie Armstrong and tell him she was having dinner with someone and he'd say, Enjoy—see you next week. But she shook her head. Jarad wasn't asking her for a 'date' date. 'You don't want to take me to dinner,' she spoke her thoughts out loud. 'What is it you do want? Are your mother and sister...?'

'Giving me a hard time? You could say that,' Jarad took up. 'In the last month I've had two visits and half a dozen phone calls. Merren, my old retainer,' he said humorously, 'I need your help.'

She wasn't sure about the 'old retainer' bit. 'That's what I'm here for,' she answered willingly. 'You should have contacted me before. I'd have come over and...'

'I was able to handle that,' Jarad cut in. 'I told Mother and Veda you were shopping with friends—I was seeing you that night. Not a problem. But...'

'Oh, heck, you've a problem now?'

'We have,' he agreed—as if she was included! 'My mother, refusing to be fobbed off—and don't think I haven't tried—and having waited until I'd finished saying how you and I were looking forward to a day of doing absolutely nothing tomorrow—is insisting I take you down to Hillmount to tea.'

'To tea?' Merren wasn't happy. 'Your mother insisted even though you'd said...'

'I got the "Surely you're not so selfish you can't spare an hour of a totally free Sunday, to introduce Merren to your father?" treatment.'

'Oh, Jarad—I don't know.' Merren began to voice her doubts.

'What don't you know?'

She rubbed a worried forefinger against her dainty chin. 'It's—different, isn't it? I mean, it's one thing to dash over to your place at short notice to keep up the pretence that we're an "item", but it doesn't seem at all right to enter your parents' home and act out that deception.'

'I can see your point, and I appreciate it. But basically we'd be deceiving them anyway—be it my place or theirs.'

'You're right, of course,' she mumbled. 'But I'd feel I was abusing their hospitality.'

'With luck we'll only be there the hour. And it's not as if you'll be expected to throw your arms around me and kiss me every seven minutes.'

'One must be thankful for small mercies,' she sniffed—and he laughed. And—he just had that effect on her—she laughed too.

'I'll call for you at two, then?' he asked.

'I'll—be ready,' she agreed, and, the tea cups empty, they stood up.

Merren guessed, having got what he'd come for, that Jarad would now go. But, to her surprise, he delayed and caught a light hold of her by her upper arms. 'I know you're sensitive, Merren, but try not to worry. I promise I'll look after you,' he said.

Looking up into his good-looking face, she felt lost for words suddenly. Then she heard a car on the drive, and immediately took a step away from him. 'You'd better come and meet *my* father,' she said, and, in panic suddenly, she urged, 'Don't mention that two thousand pounds to either my father or my brother!'

Jarad's look said, Would I? and her panic began to subside. 'Your father doesn't know you wanted the money for your brother?' he asked.

'My father knows nothing about the money!' she exclaimed in hushed tones. And, on a gasp, 'I didn't say to you that I wanted it for my brother!'

'Sweet Merren, you didn't have to. I'm neither blind nor deaf. Nor so dim-witted that I haven't realised those outstanding bills you spoke of were not yours but your brother's.'

She opened her mouth to protest, to deny, but couldn't—and, anyhow, her father and brother were by then within hearing distance. So she smiled and turned to her male kin, and introduced her friend Jarad.

Bother *her* feelings! 'Is that Jag yours?' her father asked Jarad.

'She's a beauty!' Robert exclaimed, and, before she knew it, all three men were out in the street, examining the Jaguar's long sleek lines.

Feeling blowed if she'd follow them, Merren went indoors. If Jarad Montgomery had anything else he wanted to say to her, he knew where she was. Not that he would. He'd got what he'd come for—her agreement to pay a visit to his parents tomorrow, so why would he bother coming back to say goodbye?

He didn't. Her father came in, her brother came in, but of Jarad Montgomery there was no sign. Wondering why she should feel so peeved that he had just got into his Jaguar and had purred off—it wasn't in her nature to be peeved; well, it hadn't been until she'd met *him*—Merren got on with doing yet another general tidy-up.

'Where did you meet your friend Jarad Montgomery?' her father questioned at the first opportunity.

'I met him through his brother,' she answered.

'At a rough guess, I'd say he was loaded?' he persisted, and Merren felt sick in her stomach that clearly the Jaguar, the very air around Jarad which spoke of him not being short of a penny or two, had so plainly impressed her father.

She was glad to meet up later with Bertie Armstrong and a few other friends. They were so uncomplicated, somehow, when her life just now was getting just a touch complicated, not to say confusing. Her agreement with Jarad had been meant only where his mother and sister were concerned, but now suddenly his father was included—so she rather enjoyed 'uncomplicated'.

Merren was ready and waiting when the Jaguar pulled up outside the following day. She did not have too many clothes, but those she had were of good quality. It was a warm day and her straight-skirted, short-sleeved dress of lemon silk was the obvious choice.

Her father opened the door to Jarad, just beating Queenie and Kitty for the privilege—he could be swift on his feet, her father, when he wanted to be—but Merren had no desire to delay. 'Hello,' she smiled at Jarad. 'Bye,' she told her family—and found they were all coming out to the car with her anyway.

'Lemon becomes you,' Jarad commented once they were on their way.

'You're suggesting I'm a little on the acid side?'

'Oh, my word—your sleepless nights are getting to you,' he murmured, and, while she was starting to feel a degree shamefaced, 'If I may start again—beautiful though you are, Miss Shepherd, today, in lemon, you're looking particularly beautiful.'

Her heart gave a ridiculous little flip because Jarad thought her beautiful. But a girl had to keep her feet firmly planted on the ground, so, 'Get off!' she scorned, and he laughed, and she immediately felt better.

She guessed the journey would take up to a couple of hours, and found, strangely, when she'd been feeling all uptight inside about the deception she was about to abet, that sitting beside Jarad she was feeling more relaxed and carefree than she had in a long while.

That was, she was feeling quite relaxed until casually he flicked a glance at her and remarked, 'We'd better get to know each other.'

'I trust you're not suggesting anything improper.' She attempted to nip that in the bud before he got started.

'You're a riot!' he declared—but not before she'd seen his lips twitch. 'Let me rephrase that,' he went on. 'While I know that you're a "good girl", and haven't yet, but that you're working on it, I believe that in our efforts not to be rumbled before we start our return journey, you should fill me in on anything I should be likely to know.'

'You know everything!'

'So where do you work?'

'I take your point,' she was forced to accept. 'I'm secretary to Dennis Chapman at an electronic design company. Improved Designs,' she filled in that blank. 'You may have heard of them?'

'An up-and-coming company,' he stated. 'Do you enjoy working there?'

'Very much,' she replied, and felt she could agree with anything he asked about her work.

Only, having filed away what he needed to know in that area, he then probed, more gently, it had to be said, 'Your mother died almost a year ago?'

'She was the innocent victim of a novice driver,' Merren stated, glancing out of the side window but not seeing the view.

'It must have hurt you to part with her ring.'

'I...' she began, having forgotten she had told him about selling her mother's ring. But... 'This—I don't think this comes under the heading of "Things I need to know".' She got herself more of one piece.

'So,' he accepted, 'what does your father do?'

A good question. 'Do?' she prevaricated.

'His job, his profession?'

He was being very patient! Merren was certain he knew she was fully aware of what he meant without that last question. 'At the moment, he—um—doesn't do anything in particular.'

'He can't be retired?'

Her father was fifty-two. Why did she feel she had to defend him? Because he was her father, that was why, even though, having walked out on her mother when Merren was so small, he had not been a father to her since then—if before.

'What does your father do?' she countered, but as a deflective weapon it didn't get off the ground.

'He's one of the country's leading child-psychologists,' he answered. 'He's retired now, but is still regularly consulted.' But, not veering an iota from his course, he continued, 'With neither your brother nor your father working, you must be the only one with a job in your household.'

'I never said that!' she objected.

'You're the only one bringing a salary home,' he went on. 'You're supplementing the income for a family of seven.'

Ooh, if only she didn't owe him two thousand pounds! She'd get out of this car and crawl home if she had to. 'I'll bet your father had a field-day child-psychoanalysing you!' she snapped waspishly—and could have hit him when, turning sideways to glare at him, she could have sworn she saw him suppressing a smile—every bit as though she had amused him! She'd had it with him! 'Anyhow,' she went on belligerently, 'you've obviously been dropping my name into your conversations with your mother—as you mentioned you might—I'd better know what you've said about me.'

'What would I say but that you're sweet, delightful...' He paused. 'And with not a bad-tempered bone in your body.'

She'd like to break a few of his! Merren took a deep and steadying breath. This man was getting to her, and she didn't like it. Normally she didn't have a pugilistic thought in her head, yet here she was thinking in terms of breaking a few of his bones! What on earth was happening to her?

'What should I know about you?' she made an effort to ask nicely.

'Ask anything,' he invited.

And she realised she knew quite a bit. He had a brother and a sister, lived in a super house in a smart part of London. She knew he was on the board of Roxford Waring. Surely that was enough to get her through an hour at his parents' home?

Though, since Jarad was plainly waiting to answer anything she might have thought of, she found one question, and asked, 'Your women-friends? I gather you've got them by the dozen—should I know anything about them?'

'Sweet Merren.' He patted her knee—she'd hit him yet! 'I'm sure I can promise that neither my mother nor my father would dream of referring to any of the women-friends in your presence. And I,' he added, 'certainly wouldn't be such a rotter as to do so.'

He was playing with her—teasing her, she knew. And she supposed it was a stupid question anyway—anyone would think she was interested in the wretched man! Pfff! Of course his parents wouldn't bring up some other female's name while she was there!

They completed the rest of the journey to Hillmount with not very much more being said. But as they pulled up on the drive, so Merren felt less and less happy about what she was doing—about what, she reminded herself, she was being paid to do.

Hillmount was a beautiful old house set in its own grounds. Merren had thought her detached home quite large—well, it had been until the rest of her family had moved in—but Hillmount was about three times the size of her home.

Feeling decidedly nervous, knowing that above all else she mustn't let Jarad down, she was heartened that when he came and opened the passenger door he took a hold of her hand, and kept holding it.

'Don't worry,' he smiled down at her. 'Everything will be fine.'

Then he was escorting her into the large house and his parents were coming to greet them: his mother so welcoming, his father tall, like Jarad, but quiet, Merren discovered, and with a glint of gentle humour seeming to be ever-present in his eyes.

Over the next hour, as Helen Montgomery presided over the teacups, conversation flowed easily and unstiltedly, and Merren started to relax. She knew it was her hostess's naturally pleasant manner that was responsible, and she began to not only warm to her, but to like her also.

It didn't seem as if Mrs Montgomery was prying, but that it was quite normal that she should enquire if Merren had a job. Though Merren didn't get to answer herself. For, just as if he'd known for ages where she worked, and hadn't only been acquainted with the details on the way down, it was Jarad who responded to the question.

'Merren has the nerve to work for a rival company,' he told his mother.

'Rival!' Merren exclaimed. 'Hardly!' And Jarad grinned at her—and she wished she could tell if that grin was true, or phony, for their onlookers' benefit, because a genuine grin like that could make a girl forget all her mother had taught her. Merren blinked—heavens, what was she thinking of!

Having tossed that thought to its rightful place—the

bin—Merren chatted to Jarad's parents, and sometimes just to his mother, while Jarad and his father discussed the engineering field.

It was near the end of their visit, when Mrs Montgomery mentioned that Jarad had told her that her mother had died. 'I'm so sorry,' she sympathised. 'You're young to have to come to terms with losing her, and I'm sure her death is still painful to you. But you have other family you live with,' she added sensitively.

'A lovely family,' Jarad put in, having tuned in to their conversation.

'You've met all of Merren's family?' his mother asked, showing a deciding interest, because it seemed her happy bachelor son was apparently very much involved with Merren.

'All except Merren's uncle Amos,' Jarad answered.

But the words had hardly died on his lips than his mother was saying, 'Then Merren must come and meet all of your family.'

'You can't wish that on her!' Jarad's father chipped in, and, at his wife's look, retreated with a chuckle.

'As I was saying,' Helen Montgomery resumed, only this time she was talking to Merren not Jarad, 'you might care to know some of Jarad's family.' She paused, obviously waiting for a reply.

Since she had to say something, and couldn't very well reply that she didn't care too much for the idea—why wasn't Jarad coming in to help her out?—Merren was left saying the only thing she possibly could say. 'I'd like to,' she murmured.

And found she was going hurtling down a road she didn't want to go when Mrs Montgomery beamed a smile, and said, 'Jarad's great-aunt Octavia will be eighty in two weeks' time. We're giving a dinner party for her.

You must come down. All the family will be here.' She was to extend this deception to the whole family? No way! Merren waited for Jarad to say something. He didn't. 'You will come with Jarad, won't you?' Mrs Montgomery insisted.

'Thank you. N...' The refusal hovered. Mrs Montgomery took her 'Thank you' as an acceptance.

'Wonderful!' she beamed, and was already making further plans, it seemed, when she went warmly on, 'Jarad's staying overnight. You will too, of course,' she continued, and even if Merren could have thought of a way out of it Helen Montgomery was so enthusiastic Merren didn't see how she could have got a word in anyway. And Jarad was still saying nothing.

Merren was still feeling stunned when they said goodbye to Helen and Edward Montgomery, who had come out to wave them off.

'A week next Saturday!' Jarad's mother reminded blissfully as Jarad turned the key in the ignition.

Merren smiled and waved, but was glad to get on the main road so she could let her smile slip. What a disaster! What an unmitigated disaster! For several miles Merren fumed. She should never have agreed to come today. She never should have. But what else could she have done? She owed him.

Nothing was coming from his side of the car, and there wasn't so much traffic about he had to concentrate *that* hard on his driving.

A few more miles on and Merren was starting to realise that she wasn't the only one in the car who was fuming. Oh, heck, Jarad had only taken her on a flying visit today to keep his mother sweet. An hour they could both cope with, just about. But what had she done? Only gone and accepted his mother's invitation to stay, not only to dinner, but overnight, and most likely for breakfast as well! Without a doubt, the happy bachelor was furious!

'It's not my fault!' she erupted, apropos of nothing.

'It isn't?'

For a man who was furious, his tone was very mild. Merren didn't trust it. 'Why didn't *you* say something?' If it was to be war, she wanted her salvo in first.

His answer, initially, was to steer the car into a lay-by and switch off the ignition. Then he turned and looked at her. 'Want a row?' he enquired pleasantly.

He didn't *look* angry. If anything, he looked more amused by her going off half cocked than anything. 'Who better to argue with?' she snapped.

'Apparently it was something I didn't say?'

'You saw the way the conversation was going!' she blasted off again. 'You knew all about the birthday weekend. Why didn't you butt in and…?'

He butted in then. 'I was mesmerised by your beauty,' he stated.

'Cut it out, Montgomery!' she flew.

'You're quite lovely,' he said softly, and, while she was the one who was mesmerised this time, he leaned forward and, otherwise not touching her, gently kissed her.

It was such a tender and quite wonderful kiss, and left Merren, her heartbeat racing, having to grapple really hard to find some composure. 'Wh-what was that for?' she managed when she'd got her breath back.

Jarad smiled. 'Don't you ever do anything on impulse?'

'I—thought you were furious, angry with me.'

'How could I be? My mother wasn't ready to hear Thank you, but no, from either you or me. If anyone's to blame, it's me. You've far more right to be furious than I.'

Merren stared at him. Was he super, or was he super? 'Talking of lovely,' she said, a smile breaking, 'you're not so bad yourself.'

'Do I get a kiss?' he enquired, and Merren had to laugh.

'I didn't say you were *that* good,' she grinned, but was unsmiling as she asked him seriously, 'Will you take care of explaining why I won't be there at your great-aunt's dinner?'

Jarad stared seriously back at her, his grey eyes steady on her deeply blue ones. 'Leave it with me. I'll think of something,' he promised, and turned from her and started up the car.

But—and she admitted it was totally ridiculous, having been at pains to avoid going again to Jarad's parents' house—Merren found on the drive home that she was half wishing that she *was* spending that dinner party weekend at Hillmount—with their elder son.

CHAPTER FOUR

JARAD MONTGOMERY was very much in Merren's mind in the week that followed. She wished she could stop thinking about him, but he was there in her head at work, at home. There while she cooked, cleaned, washed and ironed and generally tidied up for her family who—grown-ups as well as children—wouldn't know a coat hook if it jumped off the wall and bit them.

Life was dull, she admitted, and she couldn't remember it having been quite so dull before. Before what? Before she'd met Jarad? Probably, she supposed. Jarad certainly set her adrenalin going, be it when she was rearing up at him—she'd never used to be like that either—or when he had kissed her.

That kiss! Oh, heavens—he hadn't even touched her, save for placing his super mouth over hers—and even now she felt all wobbly.

'Are you seeing Jarad tonight?' her father asked on Saturday morning.

'Not tonight,' she replied. 'I'm seeing Bertie and...'

'You're never seeing Bertie Armstrong in preference to Jarad Montgomery?' her father questioned, scandalised. And before she could tell him that chance would be a fine thing, he was saying pithily, 'You must be mad! Jarad Montgomery's rich enough to give you everything you'd ever need, while Bertie Armstrong doesn't look...'

'You think money's so important I should only go out with men who have it?' Merren interrupted, scandalised herself that her father should think that way.

'Well, the pittance you bring in isn't going very far,' he grumbled nastily, and Merren felt her newly discovered temper—which so far had seemed to be targeted solely on Jarad—start fraying at the edges. She knew she was on the brink of telling her father that her 'pittance' might go further if he'd thought of paying back the ten pounds he'd 'borrowed' from her last Friday, *and* another ten pounds she'd lent him the Friday before that. 'I think I'll go and see Uncle Amos.'

Her father didn't answer, so she collected the cake and went out to her car. She mustn't quarrel with her father; she mustn't. But he was showing no sign of either moving back to Cornwall or looking for a job. Robert seemed to have lost heart about looking for a job too. And Carol, who truly struggled to give her children standards, seemed to be on the verge of giving up altogether and was frequently in tears. They were all out right now, in her father's car—he had said that if they were all going out, he'd stay in and enjoy some peace and quiet.

'How are things where you live?' Uncle Amos asked cheerfully when he saw her.

'Couldn't be better,' she lied, wishing she could come and live with him—at least then she'd have a bed of her own.

'You *are* all right for money?' He wanted to be sure.

The darling! His chair, though comfortable, was threadbare, as was most of his furniture. 'Absolutely!' she assured him brightly.

'You would say, if you weren't?' he insisted. 'I know you have your pride, but I *am* family, and I could help...'

'Oh, sweetheart! Stop worrying. We're fine, honestly!' She smiled, and if she hadn't loved him so much would have loved him some more because, when church mice could be no poorer, he would have beggared himself some more to help her out.

She enjoyed her visit to her uncle, and reflected on the way home on how the wish had come unbidden that she could move to her uncle's home. That wish, however, started her wondering about moving out of the house she had grown up in and moving into a small flat on her own. But how could she move out? Apart from the fact that prior to everyone moving in she had enjoyed living where she did, poor Carol was growing more and more dependent on her just lately.

By Wednesday of the next week dull had become deadly dull. Jarad had obviously given his mother some successful excuse for why one Merren Shepherd would not be at his great-aunt Octavia's dinner party on Saturday. There was every likelihood, Merren mused, that she would never see him again.

She did see him again, though. The very next day—in print! She had been working late, as she sometimes did, and was on the point of going home when, taking some papers in to Dennis Chapman's office, she glanced at the early edition of the evening paper spread open on her employer's desk. She flicked a glance at it, and stopped, rooted. There, staring back at her, was Jarad Montgomery! Riveted, Merren made a closer inspection. He looked more handsome than ever in his evening suit, pictured as he— and companion—made their way into some charity concert.

Merren didn't want to look at the gorgeous female hanging on his arm, but she did. A sick kind of feeling invaded her as she looked at the willowy, sleekly gowned brunette—a sick feeling which Merren decided was obviously due to the fact that she was working late and was probably overdue something to eat.

'Ah, you've got those letters ready for me!' Dennis Chapman smiled, coming back into the room.

Merren came away from his desk, but carried that picture with her all the way home. The woman was named Isadora Thomas, and she had been smiling as she'd clung on to Jarad.

Strangely, when Merren had thought she must be hungry, she discovered she had no appetite when she arrived home. Which was perhaps just as well, because Carol hadn't yet started on the meal but handed the crying baby Samuel over to her and started verbally on her husband instead. Their two female offspring began to quarrel too—and, to complete the bedlam, the phone rang.

'I'll answer it!' shrieked Queenie.

'No, I will!' Kitty squealed.

Merren was nearer; she settled it by picking up the phone herself. 'Hello?' she answered.

'Are you free to talk?' Jarad asked as a loud argument broke out between her two nieces and Samuel hollered in Merren's other ear. 'I can hear that you're not,' his voice penetrated through the din. 'I'll come over.'

No, unless you're going out? she noticed. 'I'll break my date!' she snapped, and put the phone down, separated Kitty's hands from Queenie's hair, and wondered what was the matter with her that when she had felt extraordinarily pleased to hear Jarad's voice, she should snap at him so vinegarily?

An hour later and peace had been restored. That was, the two girls had gone to bed, as had Carol, Robert was doing his pathetic best to cope with his fretful son, while Lewis Shepherd had taken himself off, with a further loan from Merren, down to the pub.

Merren had by then changed into jeans and a shirt, and had given herself a lecture on not snapping for snapping's sake. How could she snap at Jarad? Were it not for him those bills would still be unpaid, and Lord knew what would have happened. The threat Robert had been under, of a visit from the bailiffs, had not been idle.

Since one never knew when bedlam was likely to break out again, Merren watched for Jarad to arrive from the sitting room window. She went outside as soon as she saw the jaguar, and met him as he was unlatching the garden gate.

'You're welcome to come in, but any talking you want to do, stands every chance of getting interrupted once my nieces spot your car from their bedroom window.'

'We'll talk in my car,' he decreed, and escorted her out to it. 'I trust you managed to break your date?' he enquired silkily, not risking being pursued by the terrible two, and pulling away from the kerb.

'For you, anything,' she said sweetly.

'As it should be,' he murmured—and she didn't know whether to laugh, or hit him.

Jarad drove on for a little while before turning off down a country road, and then to a lane, where he pulled in to the side and turned off the engine. Then, as Merren turned to look at him, he turned in his seat and looked at her.

'How have you been?' he enquired casually.

'Can't complain. Yourself?' she countered.

'I'm—um—in *big* trouble,' he confessed.

'Well, if you will have your picture taken with your arms all around some ravishing beauty!'

Jarad let the exaggeration go. 'You saw it? So did my mother!'

'Oops. Your mother's been in touch?'

'She rang—two minutes before I rang you.'

'You're in panic,' Merren accused. 'Was it in the later editions of the paper?'

'She didn't get the paper. Wesley, my sister's husband, took the paper home. Veda, bless her heart, faxed the picture on to her mother.'

'You *are* in trouble,' Merren said cheerfully. 'They're all ganging up on you.'

'You can say that again!'

'So now you've decided you've had enough, and you've come to tell me you and I are through and that you're going to tell your mother—' Merren broke off. 'Why would you bother coming to tell me that? There was no "you and I" to start with. And...'

'I love your brain,' he drawled.

She ignored him—she was still trying to work out why he had come to see her, trying to work out what it was he thought they had to 'talk' about. 'Ah!' Light dawned. 'I still owe you. Whatever happens, I'm still in your debt. A debt...'

'Talking of owing, talking of working off that debt...' Jarad smiled charmingly—she didn't trust it. 'I confirmed to my tenacious parent that we'll both be going down to Hillmount on Saturday.'

'*Both!*' Merren knew she had been right not to trust that smile. But, even while her brain was telling her differently, she just wasn't ready to accept what she thought he was telling her. 'You mean you and the brunette? You and Isadora...?' Jarad's suddenly amused look caused her to break off.

'Come, come, Merren,' he mocked, 'you know better than that.'

'No!' she said positively. Then she checked. 'You mean—to stay overnight?'

'You and me, to stay overnight,' he confirmed.

'No. Definitely no.' It didn't require any thinking about.

'You've nothing to worry about,' Jarad assured her.

'Your *whole* family will be there!' she objected—and, referring to family, remembered her own, and what they owed him. Correction, what she owed him. Which, she inwardly sighed, was what this—Jarad being here—was all about. 'Was your mother very upset?'

'About the picture? Outraged,' he answered. 'And certain if I don't mend my ways that I'll lose you.'

Oh, crumbs! 'You still want to go on with this—this pretence, that you and I are serious about each other?'

Jarad stared into her worried blue eyes. 'I do,' he answered quietly. And, bracingly, 'What are you so worried about?' he asked, but his tone had toughened when, startling her by the change, he added, 'You're not seriously attached to this man you've been seeing?'

'Probably about as serious as you are about Isadora Thomas!' she flew—grief, what was the matter with her?

Jarad's look was hostile for a few seconds, and then silkily he smiled. 'If that's the case, you can have no objection on those grounds to coming with me to Hillmount.'

So, apparently, he was not the slightest serious about Isadora? Merren admitted she was starting to feel better than she had, but owned, 'Given that I'm up to my neck in them, I'm not at all happy with deception and lies, Jarad. Couldn't you just impress on your mother, on your sister—any of your mother's aiders and abetters—the truth? Can't you get them to see you're having a wonderful time just being on your own—single—and that you don't want to change that?'

'I've tried. Believe me, I've tried,' Jarad replied. And then his tone was softening, and coaxing, as he dangled a nice fat carrot. 'Think of it, Merren,' he tempted, 'you'd have a proper bed to sleep in.'

A proper bed! She could say goodbye to that sofa for one night. 'Oh, don't!' she wailed. 'It sounds—' She broke off, a shadow crossing her features.

'What's wrong?' Jarad at once demanded.

She was reluctant to tell him, but realised that, in the circumstances, she would have to. 'I—er—might be a bit of a nuisance,' she felt bound to confess.

Jarad stared at her, all too obviously none the wiser. 'Nuisance?'

'I s-sometimes, not always but sometimes, have nightmares. I wake myself up yelling,' she explained. 'I wouldn't want to disturb your parents if they're light sleepers, or any other of their guests.'

She had lowered her eyes, feeling awkward at having to tell him that, but when she flicked a glance back up at him, she saw only understanding in the grey eyes that looked back at her. 'Have you always had nightmares?' he asked. She shook her head. 'How long has it been going on?' he questioned quietly.

Merren had no trouble at all in remembering. 'The first one happened that night I was mugged,' she replied, and unexpectedly found he had taken her hand in his.

'You poor love,' he sympathised. 'Have you seen anyone about them?'

'A counsellor, you mean?' she asked, feeling choked for a moment by the warmth and sudden kindness she felt emanating from him. 'I don't think there's any need. The nightmares are less frequent than they were. And I wouldn't have mentioned them at all. It's just that, in a strange bed, a house different from my own, add a sprinkling of nerves and I'm sure Saturday night will see me yelling the place down.'

'You're coming with me, then?' he asked.

'You knew I would!' How could she not go with him? She owed him. 'Is there a chance I could have a room in an out-of-the-way corner, do you think?' she asked earnestly.

'It's really upsetting you, isn't it?' he commiserated gently. 'Leave it with me,' he added, and another un-thought of complication just then struck her.

'Your mother won't expect us to sleep together, or anything tricky like that, will she?' she asked in a rush— and Jarad burst out laughing.

'Oh, Merren, did I say you were a riot?' She guessed she was in for some tormenting. 'Put your maidenly blushes away,' he teased. 'I think I can definitely promise that, while my mother does her best to keep up with modern trends, she's not taken that one on board yet.'

What could she say? She knew her colour was a little pink. 'May I have my hand back, please?' she requested.

Jarad let go her hand and, the issue settled, he drove her home. 'We needn't go down too early,' he informed her as he got out of the car and stood with her at her garden gate. 'Will you be back from visiting your uncle Amos if I call around three?'

Merren liked him. He seemed to know that to visit her uncle was important to her. 'Fine,' she smiled.

'Till then,' he bade her. 'And don't worry.'

Merren went indoors and strangely slept better that night. Friday night, before she went to bed, was a bit of a strain, though. She waited until the girls were safely upstairs and asleep, and Samuel was having a rest from crying, and announced to her father, her brother and Carol, that she would not be there the next night.

'Going somewhere nice?' Robert asked, but before she

could answer, 'I wanted to borrow your car!' he exclaimed heavily. 'I was going to ask, only…'

'You may have it. I—er—won't need it.'

'Somebody's picking you up?' Her father cottoned on straight away. 'It's to be hoped you're not going away for the weekend with Bertie Armstrong!' Suddenly his tone became shrewd, speculative. 'Or—is it Jarad Montgomery you're going away with?'

She did not like the way he made going away with Jarad for the weekend sound—he made it sound all sort of sordid, somehow. 'I'm going with Jarad, yes,' she owned. 'But to his parents. There's a family party.'

'Getting well acquainted,' her father put in.

'I'll only be away tomorrow night.'

'You go and enjoy yourself, Merren.' Carol smiled, and the baby cried—and the discussion ended.

Merren went to see her uncle the next morning, and was hard put to know how to answer when he asked, as he did sometimes, if she was going anywhere special that night.

She would have liked to tell all about Jarad, but to do so would mean she would have to tell him about the money, and from his remarks last Saturday she knew it would only distress him if he had any idea of how deeply in Jarad's debt she was.

But since she had no way of knowing if—as unlikely as it seemed—her father might take it into his head to pay her uncle a visit, she told him that she had met a very nice man. 'We're only friends,' she inserted hastily. 'But I'm going to a family dinner party with him tonight.'

'You've kept him quiet,' Amos Yardley opined, with a twinkle in his eyes.

'Oh, we're only friends,' Merren reiterated quickly.

'And what's his name?'

'Jarad,' she said, 'Jarad Montgomery.'

'Well, he won't be good enough for you, whatever his name is,' her uncle replied, and Merren, while smiling at what he said, knew from that statement that, as she loved him, her uncle loved her.

She left him to go home and to change and to be ready for when Jarad called. It was a warm summer's day; she opted to wear a silky two-piece and packed a sleeveless ankle-length straight dress in a deep blue that matched her eyes.

She was giving her hair a last-minute comb in the bathroom when she heard Jarad arrive. From the squeals that floated up from down below, she guessed her nieces were very pleased to see him. For herself, she owned she had very mixed feelings.

Seeing her family, noisy but secure, gave Merren the boost her spirits needed when she went down to the sitting room. She looked across to Jarad and found a smile—that her family was secure was all down to him. 'Ready?' she asked.

'You've nothing to be nervous about,' Jarad assured her once they were on their way.

'Do you often take women to your family dinner parties?' she asked.

Jarad considered the question. 'Do you know, I think you're the first?' he owned, and chatted pleasantly to her all the way down to Hillmount.

Because of the easy way Jarad was with her, Merren found that any nerves she had been suffering from faded. But, the moment he turned the jaguar into the drive at Hillmount, so her nerves returned threefold.

'All right?' he asked quietly, pausing for a moment on the gravelled drive.

'Just remember, when all this blows up in your face, that it was all your idea, not mine,' Merren replied.

Jarad smiled encouragingly. 'Just try to pretend to like me,' he requested.

'No problem,' she answered, and was able to smile a natural smile.

Jarad stared at her. 'I nearly gave you another impulsive kiss then,' he murmured.

Solemnly she stared at him. 'Control yourself!' she ordered sternly—and felt her heartbeats become all fluttery when his smile became a grin.

Carrying both his overnight bag and hers, Jarad escorted her inside the house, where his mother came hurrying forward. 'How lovely to see you, Merren,' she beamed, and kissed her, and kissed her son before saying, everything going swimmingly, it seemed, 'Everyone's outside on the rear lawn. Do you want to come and say hello first, or take your things to your room?'

'We'd better come and say hello,' Jarad decreed, dropping their bags down and taking a hold of Merren's arm.

Merren supposed it was better to get it over with now than later. The sooner she met Jarad's family *en masse*, the sooner her nerves might settle. With luck, perhaps the hours until tomorrow could be got through without her having to tell any lies.

The next twenty minutes went by in a confusion of names and faces of aunts and uncles and cousins and cousins-in-law, with the guest of honour, Great-Aunt Octavia, a fine, straight-baked specimen of an eighty-year-old, holding court.

'We'll see you later,' Jarad said affably, when all the politeness had been observed, and guided Merren back to where he had left their bags.

Not one question requiring her to lie had been uttered,

and she began to relax a little. While still not feeling any
happier about deceiving any of Jarad's family, Merren
began to see that his family, as with most people, were
just too well mannered to ask point-blank any awkward
questions. And anyhow, if any of them had seen that
picture in the paper of him and Isadora Thomas, they
would know that there was nothing serious going on between Jarad and herself, the woman he had brought with
him.

'This way,' he said easily, but walked past the main
staircase to the end of the hall and down a side hall,
where a less grand staircase came into view. 'We're in
the old servants' quarters,' he said lightly, and Merren,
guessing that all the bedrooms in the house would be
occupied this weekend, went up the stairs with him.

The house was eighteenth-century, and had, she realised, been extensively modernised. The bedroom Jarad
took her to was not over-large, but what it lacked in size
it made up for in charm.

'I think that you'll be comfortable here,' Jarad commented evenly.

'I'm sure I will,' Merren answered, and suddenly realised her room was in a wing that was apart from the rest
of the house 'Oh, Jarad,' she said softly, 'your mother's
given me this room especially, hasn't she?'

'We're both in this wing,' he answered.

'Oh, I'm sorry,' she apologized. 'You were evicted
from your usual room so that I shouldn't be in this part
of the house by myself.'

'With so many aunts and uncles staying overnight, I'd
already volunteered my room,' he answered cheerfully.

'What did you tell your mother?' Merren wanted to
know, her expression unsmiling as she thought of the
trouble she must have put Mrs Montgomery to.

'What would I tell her? I told her the truth.'

'*You've* changed!'

'And you're getting upset.'

'I shouldn't have come. Your mother's got enough to do without finding me somewhere out of the way to...'

'From her point of view, with all the clan descending, it's probably solved a problem of where to put us,' Jarad interrupted. 'While I know she would have preferred you to have the best room in the house, one or two of the older relatives are starting to creak a bit, and my mother had to do a balancing act.'

'Balancing against fit and able.'

'Exactly. When I told her that you'd been mugged and were still having nightmares from it—given that she'd have come and given you a big hug to make you better if she could—this wing was the answer to your night-time serenading.' His term 'night-time serenading' for her yelling out while in the throes of a nightmare made her smile, and, seeing her smile at last, 'That's better,' Jarad said softly.

'I've been a bit of a pain, haven't I?' she said.

'Not at all,' he disagreed. 'You're a warm, sensitive and truthful woman, who's had to go against a lot of her natural instincts just lately. I wish I could make things better for you,' he added.

'You already have,' Merren began. 'Your generosity with that money...' Her voice tailed off when she suddenly noticed that there were two other doors in the room. One, she gathered, led to an adjoining bathroom. But—the other? 'What's through there?' she asked.

Jarad didn't bother turning to look. She supposed he had no need to. 'Um—I was afraid you might ask that,' he replied. His words brought suspicion to her mind. With her eyes fixed on his, she said nothing—but waited.

'It leads to my room,' he continued after a moment, and got the rest of it said and done with when, holding her unsmiling blue glance steady, he revealed, 'I'm afraid that, over the years, the key has become lost.'

Merren stared at him. 'Leaving the door locked or unlocked?'

Jarad stared back. 'Unlocked,' he replied.

Merren took a steadying breath. Her relationship with Jarad was purely platonic; she knew that. Was purely expedient from his happy-bachelor stance; she knew that too. But—and she faced that at twenty-two she was perhaps a little—um—late developing—but when it came to it, she didn't seem to know much else at all.

She, Merren mused wretchedly, just didn't need anything else to worry about. She had to sort this out here and now—even if Jarad Montgomery did bust a rib laughing.

'You wouldn't…?' The words stuck. She swallowed. 'You—er—know more about these things than me. You—er—wouldn't…?' Her voice went all choky.

'Wouldn't?' Jarad encouraged.

She had an idea he was playing with her. She didn't like it. 'I have your word as a gentleman that you won't start any—um—funny business?' Having forced the words out, she could have hit him when he did burst out laughing.

'Funny business! Oh, little Merren, you're unbelievable.'

It was not the answer she wanted. 'I already know that,' she told him stiffly. 'What I need to know…'

'You're serious, and I'm not being very kind,' he capitulated suddenly. And his expression was as serious as hers as he went on, 'Trust me, the thought of attempting to seduce you never entered my head.' Dress it up, why

don't you? She knew she had gone pink. 'Nor,' Jarad
assured her, his glance slightly fascinated on the flush of
colour to her skin, 'is it ever likely to.'

Well, thank you very much! 'What time's dinner?' she
asked him shortly.

'We'll go down at seven,' he replied pleasantly.
'You'll be all right if I leave you now?'

If you never came back would be fine by me! 'Good
heavens, yes!' she exclaimed, and was glad when, with
a sharp glance to her, he left.

Merren heard him moving about in the next room, but
didn't thank him that he had departed her room by the
door out to the landing—every bit as if to say that as far
as he was concerned that communicating door between
their two rooms was as if it were locked, for he would
never use it.

She unpacked her overnight bag and mutinied against
him. Who did he think he was? He with his, 'Trust me,
the thought of attempting to seduce you never entered
my head. Nor is it every likely to.' Huh! He could jolly
well... Suddenly Merren halted mid-thought. What on
earth was the matter with her? She was feeling miffed
because, when she'd have screamed blue murder had he
attempted to seduce her, Jarad had made it exceedingly
plain that he didn't even fancy her?

Forget it, do! Count your blessings. She looked around
the room, at the wonderful bed—and her heart lifted. A
bedroom to herself. A bed. Be it only for one night—she
had a proper bed to sleep in. On impulse, she kicked off
her shoes and went and lay down on top of the bed.
Bliss—sheer, unadulterated bliss!

Fearing that she might fall asleep, however, and would
not be ready at seven, Merren went and investigated the
adjoining bathroom. Some ten minutes later she was ly-

ing luxuriating in the bath when it suddenly dawned on her that for quite some while now she had been unwound sufficiently to have ceased worrying about the dinner party that evening, and the deception she and Jarad were playing.

While she still didn't feel any better about deceiving Mrs Montgomery in particular, especially when she was accepting her hospitality, Merren couldn't help wondering, had she been rather making a mountain out of a molehill? On thinking about it, she recalled that her brother Robert had brought several female friends home before eventually he'd met Carol. So, Merren pondered, surely Mrs Montgomery would forgive her if, once the year was up, Jarad no longer mentioned her name, and brought some other girl to meet his family.

Somehow Merren wasn't happy with that last thought, but as she later brushed her pale reddish hair, with its natural streaks of blonde, she wondered—since Jarad seemed to be taking this deception so lightly—if perhaps she was guilty of making heavy weather of it.

Merren decided there and then that she was going to be more like the person she had been a year ago, before her mother had died and her world had started to crumble.

She was dressed and ready at five to seven, her hair shining and loose to her shoulders, the blue of her dress suiting her perfectly. She owned she had started to feel more cheerful, and did not have to manufacture a smile when Jarad came and knocked on her door.

She opened it, and as Jarad stood admiring her, so she couldn't help noticing how magnificent he looked in his dinner suit. 'You don't look so bad yourself,' she said lightly, as his gaze travelled the length of her and back to her laughing blue eyes.

She saw his mouth twitch, and thought for one moment that she might be on the receiving end of one of his kisses of impulse. But, whether he at that moment recalled she had been a mite anxious about any 'funny business', she didn't know, but instead he took a step away from her, and Merren felt just a shade disappointed. Disappointed? Get yourself together, girl, do!

'You're feeling calmer,' he observed, as she left her room and they fell into step.

'I'm sorry,' she apologised. 'You're not used to un-cooperative women, are you?'

'Who's been talking?' he asked mock ferociously— and she laughed.

She laughed a lot that evening. His family were close, and rather special, and she felt privileged to be among them. Faces and names began to sort themselves out through the evening, and everyone was warm and delightful to her, making her most welcome.

In particular, Franklin Blake, son of Aunt Barbara and a man about the same age as his cousin, Jarad, paid her a lot of attention. While he was not the sort of man any woman in her right mind would consider getting serious about—he already had two divorces behind him—he was extremely funny, and made her laugh a lot.

Merren renewed her acquaintance with Jarad's sister, and met Veda Partridges' husband, Wesley, and enjoyed talking to him.

Dinner was a splendid affair, with Great-Aunt Octavia the guest of honour and showing not the smallest sign of flagging, for all her eighty years. Though it was true that at half past ten, when they were all back in the drawing room, she decided that she'd had a most wonderful time but was going to bed. One of the aunts went with her, but conversation still buzzed.

Merren was sitting talking to Franklin Blake, while Jarad was getting his aunt Barbara a drink, when she wondered, this being a family party, if she should make herself scarce.

'Your mother wanted a word with you,' Jarad came over to tell Franklin.

'Do you think I should go to bed?' Merren asked Jarad as Franklin went to see what his mother wanted.

'Don't tell me you've had enough of Cousin Franklin!' Jarad said in a low tone that didn't sound very pleasant to her.

'Until a moment ago I was having a lovely time,' she snapped in likewise manner.

'Forgive me for intruding!' he snarled, and as he abruptly left her, Merren promptly decided that it was more than high time she went to bed.

She glanced across the room to her hostess, who was in some deep discussion with one of her sisters, and saw, as Jarad went to have a word with his cousin Una, that she probably wouldn't be noticed if she slipped away.

Up in her room, Merren washed and got into bed and started to mutiny against Jarad Montgomery again. Against all the odds, considering she hadn't wanted to come to Hillmount today, she had thoroughly enjoyed the family gathering. She hadn't wanted to tell lies, and was grateful she hadn't been called upon to do so. So that as the evening had progressed she had begun to enjoy herself. Well, *he* wouldn't have liked it had she sat there with a long face all evening. Would he?

Having been relaxed, all her worries about her own family temporarily forgotten, having been happy again for a few hours, Merren's spirits hit rock bottom. She'd be glad when tomorrow came and she could go home.

Let Jarad Montgomery ask her to come down here again, that's all.

She heard footsteps on the stairs—and dived for the switch on her bedside lamp, and plunged her room into darkness. The footsteps stopped outside her door. Someone tapped lightly on the wood panelling. 'Merren!' It was Jarad. She wasn't feeling very friendly towards him, and didn't answer. He wouldn't come in—he of the 'Nor is it ever likely to' non-seducing variety.

He didn't come in. After a few moments, she heard his footsteps moving away. She didn't know what he wanted, and she didn't care. Because she'd had no option, she'd come to this dinner party. She closed her eyes, the word 'option' whirling around in her head. If only she hadn't been mugged...but she didn't want to think about that.

Jarad must have gone downstairs again, she realised, because she was still awake when a couple of hours later she heard him again coming up the stairs. He didn't come to her door this time. She heard him moving around in his own room and wished she could take full advantage of this wonderful bed and go to sleep.

But life had gone flat again. She had been happy—and now she wasn't. And it was his fault. And if she hadn't been mugged she wouldn't have to think of her lack of options when it came to telling that monster next door that he needn't ask her to come down to Hillmount with him ever again, because she just wasn't coming. Unfortunately, she didn't have that option. Because she *had* been mugged. She had been hit. She had been violently assaulted. That money had been stolen. She had given up her mother's ring, the ring that had once belonged to her grandmother, and Robert had been in all kinds of trouble. And if it hadn't been for Jarad letting her have that two thousand pounds, Robert and Carol and the children would be in even more trouble.

Merren tried to climb out of the strife of her thoughts. But by the time sleep came and claimed her her father had entered the equation, and her head was as filled as her overcrowded home, and it all stemmed from her mother dying and having to sell that ring—and all for nothing, because she had been mugged.

Strangely enough, she slept dreamlessly. Though from recent habit she awoke as dawn was breaking. Merren opened her eyes and a contented smile crossed her features. The last time she'd slept in a proper bed seemed light years away. Oh, fabulous, fabulous bed. The house wouldn't be astir for ages yet—enjoy it. She closed her eyes again.

But—she was being hit! Someone wanted something from her, something she didn't want to give up. She was hit again, and she began to cry out—she was falling—and somebody was touching her. She cried out louder—and awoke on a choked gasp of breath. Still terror-stricken, she sat bolt upright, and as she opened her eyes and her world started to right itself she saw that Jarad was in the room with her. He was sitting on the bed with her and must, she started to realise, have been touching her—perhaps to try to waken her from the horrors of her dream.

She stared unspeaking into his kind grey eyes. 'Poor little love,' he murmured, and as he gathered her close to him instinctively she went into his arms.

For several seconds she felt too beaten, too shaken to say very much at all. Oddly, it seemed in no way alien that at around five o'clock on a Sunday morning she should be sitting up in bed in her 'next to nothing' nightie, being gently held against the chest of a robe-clad male. That it was Jarad who held her seemed to be right too, somehow.

But Merren, although she felt disinclined to move, was rapidly starting to get herself more of one piece. 'W-was I making much of a racket?' she asked against his chest.

Gently he stroked her hair. 'Will you not allow me to get you some help?' he asked, from which she guessed she must have been kicking up quite a din.

Merren pulled back from him, and most peculiarly wished she hadn't when he took his arms from around her. Oddly, she wanted them back where they were. 'It's not necessary,' she assured him. 'Thank you all the same. They, my dreams, are not so bad as they were.'

'*That* was better?'

'I promise it was,' she smiled, and thought Jarad a bit wonderful when he stretched out his arms and gathered her to him again in a sympathetic hug. She sighed against him. 'You're nice,' she said.

'You're sure you're not light-headed?'

She laughed against him—but didn't make the mistake of pulling out of his arms again. Mistake? This would never do! She pulled back. Against all her instincts she pulled out of his arms.

'I'm sorry I woke you,' she apologised.

'I was reading.'

He hadn't been asleep? 'You don't need much sleep?' she queried—they had touched on many subjects, but not this one.

'Not much,' he agreed. 'But you do. At a guess I'd say you've a lot of sleep to make up.'

'I look a wreck?' Oh, grief—why had she said that? They had been talking personally, but impersonally somehow, and what had she done but invite his personal inspection of her?

Jarad studied her face, leaned back, and glanced to where the thin strap of her nightdress had fallen down one arm, glanced to where the fine silk barely covered her breasts—and back up to her face again.

'In point of fact, Miss Shepherd, you must be the only woman I know who could go without sleep for a week— and still look outrageously beautiful.'

Merren blinked, looked at him. His gaze was steady— he seemed sincere. *'Moi?'*

'Vous. Didn't you know?' She shook her head, her heart beating nineteen to the dozen suddenly that Jarad thought her beautiful—outrageously so. A smile began somewhere inside of her. It made it to her mouth. She saw Jarad's glance go down to her smile. 'You're looking happier,' he observed. 'Do you want me to stay a while longer—or are you ready to finish out your sleep?'

She wanted him to stay a while longer. 'I think I'm ready for sleep,' lied she who had hated the thought of having not to tell the truth. To compound her lie, she lay down.

Jarad went to pull the clothes up around her—but accidentally brushed his hand across her breast. She stared at him, more startled by the tingle that shot through her than anything.

'Sorry!' Jarad apologised at once, on seeing her startled expression. 'I wasn't starting any "funny business", I promise.'

Merren had to laugh at his use of her expression. 'I know,' she assured him, her mouth curving upwards.

And Jarad smiled. 'Whoever gets you is going to be one hell of a lucky man,' he observed, and, bending forward, he lightly kissed her, and, via the communicating door through which he must have sped on hearing her crying out, he left.

Merren lay awake for a long while after he'd gone. She did like him, she realised. She really liked him. They had not parted the best of friends last night. But, on hearing her distress as she'd started yelling in her nightmare, he hadn't hesitated to come in, all enmity forgotten.

She owned that she had forgotten her own anger towards him. It hadn't seemed to matter when she had been in his arms. In fact nothing very much had seemed to matter then. She touched her fingers to her mouth, to the lips he had lightly saluted, and realised she quite liked his kisses of impulse.

Merren slept for a few hours, but woke up to relive all that had taken place the last time she had surfaced from sleep—and owned to be feeling very mixed up about almost everything. She recalled again how nothing had seemed to matter when she had been in Jarad's arms— and shot out of bed, as if trying not to think.

She was still not ready to take on board what, if any, were the implications to be drawn from the pleasure she'd found in being held by Jarad. She showered and dressed, and she discovered she didn't feel ready to face him again yet. Why she should feel shy to see him again, she couldn't fathom. But it was a lovely sunny morning—she decided to take herself off for a walk.

Perhaps because it was still relatively early, she didn't meet anyone as she let herself out of the house. Merren tried to keep her mind a blank as she walked, but found that extremely difficult to do. Yet, when she would have thought Robert and Carol, and their lack of harmony together, and the problems that seemed daily to beset them would take prime place in her thoughts, it was not thoughts of them that occupied her, but thoughts of Jarad.

She was out for some while, and was reluctant to return. But, manners being what they were, though breakfast would be a 'come down and help yourself when you're ready' type of meal, Merren started to retrace her steps. She might not have wanted to come to Hillmount yesterday, but certain courtesies were still owed to her hosts.

Merren was nearing the entrance to the house when the door opened, and she felt as if her heart were in her mouth. Why that should be, she had no idea, but her fast-beating heart instantly settled down again when she recognised that the man approaching her was not Jarad, but was his cousin, Franklin.

She would possibly have gone by him with a pleasant 'good morning', but Franklin Blake, it seemed, was keen to have a few words with her. 'I didn't get to say good-night to you last night,' he complained, managing to look a tinge devastated.

'It was a super evening, wasn't it?' She smiled.

'Made especially so because you were there,' he answered without having to think about it.

'You're a flirt,' she accused, not having to think about that herself.

'What I am, dear Merren, is totally smitten,' he replied.

'I hope you'll soon be better.' She didn't believe it for a moment.

'Straight up...?' he began to question.

'Yes?' she queried.

'You and Jarad—how serious is it between you and my cousin?' he wanted to know.

Merren was wary. If she said not serious at all, would he go back and tell the rest of the family? Oh, what would Jarad want her to say? 'Why do you want to know?' she prevaricated.

'Because I want to take you out. I want to...'

'Sorry.' She stopped him before he got any further.

'Sorry as in—I don't stand a dog's chance?'

'Charming though you are,' Merren answered with a soothing smile, 'I'm spoken for.'

Franklin's answer was to take hold of her left hand and kiss the back of it. 'Always the best man,' he complained. Though, since he'd been a groom twice, Merren didn't think he'd got very much to complain about.

She retrieved her hand, gave him another 'no hard feelings' smile, parted from him and headed the remaining distance to the house. She did not get very far, however, because just then the door was pulled open again and, his expression thunderous, Jarad strode out. Oh, oh, somebody was in trouble!

The surprise was that it was her. 'What the devil do you think you're playing at?' Jarad demanded, taking her by the arm and spinning her about.

'I wasn't intending to go that way!' she refused to be browbeaten—what had she done, for goodness' sake?

'And I wasn't intending to be made to look a fool.'

'By me?' she asked, startled. 'What did I do?'

'More than enough!' he grated. 'For your information, most of my family are in the drawing room, with a first-class view of you flirting with my cousin.'

'Flirting! Now just a minute. He may have...'

'You don't call holding hands with him, smiling up at him as if he's the best thing you've come across since quick-drying paint, not to...'

'Hand-holding!'

Jarad ignored her, his expression arctic. 'You're here with *me*, not him,' he reminded her. 'Here for my benefit, not his.' And, while Merren was staring, stunned, and of the opinion that she didn't need any of this, 'My mother, my aunts, my sister, most everyone else must have seen you smiling prettily while Franklin went in for a bit of hand-kissing. Just you...'

But Merren was starting to grow angry. Dammit, it seemed she couldn't win whatever she did. 'Are they still looking this way?' she interrupted him crossly.

He flicked an angry glance over her shoulder to the windows. 'Avidly!' he retorted.

Right! Without more ado Merren took a step forward, all that was needed, and, not thinking but acting, on impulse, she grabbed a hold of him and stretched up and held on to him tightly while she kissed him. Then, as she felt Jarad's hands come to her arms, and her heart started to thump, so Merren—her head beginning to whirl—let go of him and took a stunned step back. She stared at him, shaken, but if he was shaken too, he was the first to recover—Merren had a feeling that she never would. Because just then, like a lightning bolt, she suddenly knew that she loved him!

Jarad still had his hands on her arms when, looking down into her shaken expression, he drawled. 'Well, if you're going to play dirty...' and began to pull her nearer to him.

But Merren had more than enough to cope with just then without the wonderful feel of his mouth against hers again. 'Steady on, Montgomery.' She managed to find a grain of brain power from somewhere. 'Any more of that and your lovely aunts will be getting out their best wedding hats!'

She smiled; he smiled, his anger a thing of the past. His hands fell to his sides. 'You certainly know how to cool a man's ardour, Miss Shepherd,' he replied. 'Perhaps we *have* gone far enough.'

Trust her to go *too* far! Merren was still stunned by

her idiocy. All Jarad had wanted was a make-believe girl-friend to keep his mother and sister out of his hair. And what had she done? Only gone further and fallen in love with him!

CHAPTER FIVE

CHAPTER FIVE

THE hours to be got through until they would be able to leave Hillmount turned out to be not so interminable as Merren—in the light of her new-found knowledge—supposed that they would be. She urgently needed to be alone somewhere. Quite desperately did she feel a need to be somewhere by herself. But short of hiding in her room—and good manners ruled that one out—she had no wish at all for Jarad to come looking for her and maybe ask what was the matter.

Nor, she realised, would she get any privacy when she got home. Not until everyone was in bed anyhow.

Which left her with no alternative but to determine that no one should have an inkling of how catastrophic her stay at Hillmount had turned out to be. Though, on thinking about it, Merren accepted that it was true to say that the knowledge she was in love with Jarad Montgomery could have surfaced at any time, in any place, in fact, anywhere. When she thought about it, there had been enough pointers along the way.

But there was no time to think about it further, time only to mingle with Jarad's relatives, and to smile and appear happy, and to hide from any who might have eyes to see that she had recently received a shock that had rocked her to the core of her being.

'Come and take a look at my pigs,' Jarad's father invited after breakfast.

'Merren isn't interested in your herd!' Helen Montgomery admonished her husband.

'Just the two,' he answered in his quiet, amicable way, and led Merren out of the house, across a field he owned and to the last word in pig luxury.

Two pigs came out of their house and trotted up to them for a tickle. As Edward Montgomery chatted to his prize pair Merren knew it was a certainty that these pigs would die of old age—they would never become bacon.

Not that all of Edward Montgomery's conversation was reserved exclusively for the animals, for, as he and Merren stood watching them, he enquired about her family and about her work and somehow, along the way, she found he had mentioned Jarad saying she had been mugged. 'Do you feel like telling me about it?' he asked idly. Yet there was some still quietness about him that said he was truly interested to know.

In actual fact, Merren didn't want to tell him about it. What was there, in any case, to tell? She'd been knocked down, robbed—and... Somehow, and she could only ever afterwards put it down to Edward Montgomery's brilliance in the psychoanalytical area, she found that in answer to his gentle probing she was telling him not only about the mugging but how she felt inside, telling him of those locked-away feelings of being scared, of being hit and knocked to the ground, and of being angry.

When her words dried, they strolled across to a huge pond, still within his grounds, where a pair of swans glided elegantly. It was wonderfully peaceful there, and as they again started to talk on all matters it seemed as if Jarad's father was content to stay there for another hour. But suddenly he was taking a glance at his watch.

'Oh, dear!' he exclaimed. 'I've kept you away from Jarad for much too long—he's probably scouring around looking for you.'

They made their way back to the house, but Merren

knew that Jarad wouldn't come looking for her. She knew
it on two counts. One, Jarad—and she was going to have
to face up to it—had no particular interest in her. Two,
bearing in mind how only that morning Jarad had wanted
to get her some help, she was only then starting to realise
that, in all probability, he had asked his father to have a
chat with her. Jarad wouldn't come looking for her and
intrude on any conversation she was having with his leading psychologist father—who wasn't at all bad at psy-
choanalysing either!

All of which made her unsure if she wanted to speak
to Jarad again. But as she and his father entered the
house, so Jarad came out from the drawing room—
though it could be, she had to admit, that her reluctance
had just a little to do with the sudden and unexpected
shyness that took her. Oh, she did so truly love him. Her
heart started to pound just to see him—this love she bore
him, unhappily, was no figment of her imagination.

'There you are,' he said easily. 'I thought you'd got
lost.'

They left Hillmount shortly after lunch. 'You'll come
and see us again, Merren?' Helen Montgomery beamed.

What could she say? 'I'd like that,' she smiled, and
went with Jarad to his car.

They were silent for most of the drive. Merren wanted
it that way. The knowledge of her love for him was new
to her. She was terrified of saying a wrong word that
might have this astute man next to her guessing at her
secret. She hoped this would be the last occasion she
would be with him—while at the same time she felt
heartsore that it might indeed prove so.

Jarad seemed lost in his own thoughts too, for he was
very quiet. Though he did ask at one stage if her time
spent at Hillmount had been so very terrible.

'I know I wasn't supposed to enjoy it...' she began, when he cut her off.

'Where did you get that peculiar idea?' he asked abruptly, his tone showing his surprise that she should think any such thing.

She *was* supposed to enjoy it? 'So, okay, I didn't *expect* to enjoy it—er—the deception and everything. But I did.' She happened to glance at him, and saw he appeared pleased. How dear he was to...

'You liked my family?'

'They're super,' she replied.

She had thought they had finished with the subject, but, glancing at him again—she was going to have to stop doing that—she saw all good humour leave his expression as he asked shortly, 'Especially my cousin?'

Merren instinctively knew he was referring to his flirtatious cousin Franklin. 'Una's lovely,' she replied sweetly—and, receiving a sideways unsmiling glance for her trouble, Merren decided she didn't need a reprimand, thank you very much, and, though still on the subject of family, swiftly changed the subject matter. 'Was it your idea your father should give me a conducted tour of the pigsty?'

Jarad did not duck an answer, but his short tone had gone and his voice was quite kind when he asked, 'Has it helped?'

Merren considered his question—had talking out some of her innermost thoughts and feelings about that mugging helped? 'I don't know,' was the honest answer. Nor did she. What she did know was that, since being aware of her love for Jarad, there had been little room for anything else to occupy her thoughts.

They fell silent again, and had barely spoken half a dozen or so more words when he drew up the Jaguar outside her home. He got out of the car with her, and, feeling suddenly close to despair that she might never see him again, Merren wanted to put off that moment of parting. She wanted to invite him in, but realised the house would probably be in one big untidy heap—and besides, it wouldn't be just her and him then; Queenie and Kitty would want to take over.

So she smiled, and held out her hand for the overnight bag he'd taken from the boot. 'Until next time,' she remarked casually.

Jarad stood looking at her, and her heart pounded. And pounded more vigorously when his head started to come down. She stood rooted. And—he lightly kissed her cheek. She could have been one of his elderly aunts. 'Take care,' he bade her smoothly—she could have been his elderly *great*-aunt!

Merren turned from him, mutinous yet tearful, and opened the garden gate. She didn't look back. The car was being driven away before she'd so much as opened the rear door to her home.

The kitchen was a mess, the house chaos. Merren was glad. She needed something to do, needed to be fully occupied—she didn't want to have time to think. To think of how she had fallen in love with Jarad Montgomery, and the folly of that, because one Jarad Montgomery didn't want her love—nor anyone else's for that matter. He had made that manifestly clear.

It was Thursday before Merren had got herself anywhere near back together again from her discovery of her love for Jarad. He had been in her head before, but was now so constantly in her head that she knew the uselessness of trying to oust him. She went over and over again how she had come to fall in love with him—it barely made any sense. She'd see him harsh and angry, but also knew of his great kindness. So, okay, two thousand pounds, while being all the world to her, was probably nothing to him. But he needn't have lent her that money. Why, he'd hardly known anything about her when he'd handed over that money. That kindness had shown through last Sunday morning too, when she'd had the nightmare. And what about that same Sunday morning, she recalled, when, later, she'd grabbed a hold of him and kissed him?

What had got into her when she had done that? Merren had no idea. Though she did remember her mother saying on a few occasions, 'You can be a little rascal sometimes'—perhaps now she knew what her mother had meant.

But, whatever, that kiss had been the start of it. The start of knowing that life would never be the same again. The start of wondering constantly—what was Jarad doing now? The start of that dreadful monster jealousy—who was he with? Though it was fair to say, as she recalled that sick feeling she'd experienced when she'd seen that picture of him with Isadora Thomas, that she'd known jealousy before—without being able then to put a name to it.

Merren went home that night and cooked and cleaned, and did her stint of hairbrushing and teeth-brushing patrol for her two nieces, and of baby-holding, as Carol did her best to cope while Robert seemed to hinder more than help. Neither of the Shepherd men seemed inclined to find new work, and Merren's finances were getting close to being beyond perilous.

She again had treacherous thoughts of moving out, but knew deep down that while her sister-in-law was having such a dreadful time trying to cope with her lot, removing herself from the family home and letting them all get on with it was not to be. And yet—surely Carol must have coped before they'd come to live with her? Yes, but she'd thought Robert still had a job then. And then there was baby Samuel... No, moving out was not to be.

Merren was glad when Friday evening came and she met Bertie Armstrong for a quick, uncomplicated drink down at The Bull. She had seen nor heard nothing of Jarad since they had parted on Sunday, and life had gone back to being dull—deadly dull.

She made herself brighten up on Saturday when she went to see her uncle. 'Your grass is growing,' she hinted.

'You're younger than me,' he hinted straight back.

She laughed—he was special. It wouldn't matter if she was later back than usual. Though first she made them some coffee—she'd tackle the kitchen once she'd seen to that front lawn—and spent some happy minutes in talking to her uncle on anything that came up. Although he was the only person she felt she could confide in, she didn't tell him of her love for Jarad.

But thoughts of Jarad Montgomery were with her the whole time she pushed the mower up and down her uncle's front lawn. In fact, so much was Jarad in her head that, just as she had completed her mowing efforts and stopped the machine, she straightened and looked up and saw a Jaguar car approaching and thought it was him!

When, against all odds, she saw that in fact it *was* him, so her heartbeat went into overdrive. She couldn't think, felt too paralysed to move, and just stared, stunned, when the car drew to a halt outside her uncle's cottage.

She still hadn't moved an inch when Jarad, having extracted his long length out of his car, had walked to the garden gate. By the time he'd come through it, however, and was standing on the path, seeming quite happy to stay there admiring her long length of leg in her shorts, Merren had found her voice.

'Got a problem, Mr Montgomery?' she asked, her world no longer dull.

His glance moved to her face. 'Good morning, Merren. How are you?' he mockingly rebuked her for her 'greeting'.

And still she loved him. 'I can *see* how you are, and...' with a hasty consultation of her watch '...it's five past twelve.'

'So it occurred to me...' he smiled—she melted '...that since you don't like telling lies—and I confess I'm not keen myself—I'd come and see you. So, should the need arise—though I doubt it will—I can answer my mother's grilling with the truthful fact that we've spent time together today.'

Merren allowed herself a small smile—inside she was positively beaming. 'Well—if we must spend some time together...' must? She was ecstatic! '...you'd better come in—I'll make you a coffee.'

'You've been labouring with the lawn. May I make it?'

'You haven't seen the state of my uncle's kitchen!' she declined, and, as it belatedly came to her that she had never told him where her uncle lived, 'How did you kn...?' she began.

'Your father gave me directions,' Jarad answered before she could complete her question. So he must have called at her home first!

They entered her uncle's threadbare cottage and she introduced Jarad to him—and nearly died when her uncle, instead of being surprised that some man should come to his door seeking his niece out, remarked pleasantly, 'Ah, yes, Merren told me about you—though she hasn't yet got around to telling me how dinner with your family went.' Oh, help, anyone would think it had been a dinner laid on especially so she should be introduced into his family—and it hadn't been like that!

Jarad appeared interested, and flicked a glance at her scarlet face. He smiled; she fancied she saw devilment in his smile. She didn't smile back. 'I'll get you that cup of coffee,' she said as evenly as she could, and couldn't get to the kitchen fast enough.

Because of the smallness of her uncle's home she could hear every word of what was being said in the next room. Though as she cleaned up and made three cups of coffee—courtesy demanded Jarad should not sup his alone—they could have been talking in double-Dutch for all she could understand of it. What she did realise was that Jarad and her uncle were getting on famously, and had moved on from mere pleasantries to discuss things technical in the engineering world.

She had in fact just finished adding a pot of coffee to a tray and three cups when she became aware of the silence from the next room. She went in—as she'd quickly suspected, the room was empty. Quite clearly her uncle had taken Jarad to his workshop to inspect his latest invention.

She could have called them, but decided against it. Uncle Amos would be in his element, and she could always make more coffee if this lot went cold. Meanwhile it gave her time to spruce up the kitchen.

They were away so long Merren had time not only to spruce up the kitchen, but to go outside and clear away the lawn mower cuttings and put the mower away.

It pleased her that Jarad and her uncle were getting on so well—but she'd have to go soon, and she'd seen barely anything of Jarad herself, and had absolutely no way of knowing when, if ever, she would see him again.

Ten minutes later she entered the workshop and stood watching the two men, bent over a workbench and absorbed in technical conversation. She waited for a pause, then called, 'I'm off now!'

Both men looked up. Jarad took a step towards her, but it was her uncle who, with a glance to his workshop clock, guessed apologetically, 'I suppose I've had that second cup of coffee?'

She laughed. She couldn't be cross with him. She'd told him that she and Jarad were only friends. He wasn't to know how much she would have loved to have spent this past hour in Jarad's company.

She went over to her uncle and kissed his cheek. 'See you next Saturday,' she said, and thought Jarad might be stopping. But he turned and shook hands with Amos Yardley, and thanked him for showing him round his workshop. Having said their goodbyes, Jarad went out from the workshop with her.

'Mr Yardley's an exceptionally clever man,' Jarad stated as they walked up the garden path to the front gate.

'I know,' Merren smiled. 'Er—I only told him about your family party because I wasn't sure if my father would tell him...' she blurted out in a rush, felt a fool, and added a mumbled, 'If he called.'

Jarad glanced down at her. 'That's all right, then,' he commented.

Merren had no way of knowing if he meant it or if he was perhaps a little annoyed. 'I told him we were only friends.' She tried to make things better.

'And what did he say to that?' he enquired evenly.

But suddenly Merren had had enough of being on the

defensive. 'He said you wouldn't be good enough for me!' she answered on a flare of anger.

Jarad laughed, and she fell in love with him all over again. Soon they would part, and she didn't want to part from him ever. They reached the garden gate. He had a hand on it ready to open the catch and she wanted to delay him—but she didn't know how.

But he paused for a second. 'Got a date tonight?' he enquired.

Merren shook her head. 'That was last night,' she thought to mention—perish the notion that he might consider she stayed home every night. Though, as she looked at him and saw he looked a tinge hostile, she sought desperately to lighten the atmosphere. 'You can always come to supper at my place tonight if she's turned you down,' she invited flippantly; regardless of who 'she' was, she couldn't see any female turning Jarad down. But promptly got the shock of her life when he took her up on her offer.

'What time?' he batted back at her before she could blink.

'Time?' For a couple of moments she wasn't with him. But, as colour flooded her face—and she would swear she had never blushed in her life until she'd met him— she hastened to tell him, 'I wasn't being serious!'

'Too late—I've accepted!' He refused to let her rescind the invitation. 'What time?' he repeated.

Merren stared at him, knowing already that he was probably in for the worst evening of his life if she didn't stop him from coming—while part of her wanted to wildly rejoice that she needn't say goodbye to him now and live in the bleak hope of perhaps bumping into him again some day. She needn't hope, but *could* see him tonight! The chance was there, just waiting to be grabbed.

'You don't really want to eat with us?' she questioned, prevaricating, knowing she should tell him *no way* was he coming to dinner. Unspeaking, having already accepted, he looked down into the deep blue of her eyes.

'Are those long, long lashes real?' he enquired.

He knew they were. He was close enough to see that for himself. She gave in. 'Seven o'clock,' she stated loyalty to her family preventing her from telling him what hell on earth meal times nearly always were. 'And don't dress up—you'll probably be giving a hand nursing a teething baby.'

His answer was to open the gate. Though before he would allow her to go through he murmured good-humouredly, 'Till then, sweet maid,' and, bending, he kissed her cheek.

Merren brushed past him—her heart singing. So, all right, it was just one of his kisses of impulse, and she could still have been one of his aunts for all the ardour that had been behind it. But he *had* kissed her, and at one time he wouldn't have done that. She was grateful for crumbs.

The afternoon flashed by in a flurry of activity as Merren again tidied up, and Carol—at first in a panic that they were entertaining—went on to threaten her daughters to be on their best behaviour that night.

Lewis Shepherd had a habit of finding somewhere to go every Saturday evening. But, on learning they were having company, he decided to stay home. He even asked, 'Can I give you a hand with anything?'

Merren had never heard her father make such an offer before. Nor, apparently, had anyone else, because Robert looked at him and asked, 'What do you want to borrow, Dad?' He'd meant to be humorous—his father didn't see it that way, and scowled at him.

'I can manage, thanks,' Merren said hurriedly. 'It's only one extra, after all.'

But what a one extra! She wished they were having something more imaginative than pasta and salad, but with seven of them at the table her budget wouldn't run to fillet steaks all round.

The menu, or lack of it, went completely from her mind when, with less than an hour to go before seven, Robert got on her sister-in-law's nerves as he interfered with her decision that Queenie would wear pink ribbons in her hair and like it.

Merren shut herself in the bathroom as irritation with each other escalated between her brother and sister-in-law into a full-scale row. She didn't need this, Merren thought unhappily. It was all so petty. And yet Carol was really suffering—so too was Robert, in his own way.

She sighed, guessing that Carol would be in tears by now. She wanted to help—but knew she couldn't interfere. All in all, Merren knew that her flippant 'come to supper at my place...' was the worst idea she'd ever had.

Which made it totally pleasing and surprising that—perhaps everyone on their best behaviour—the evening started off very well. Jarad arrived at precisely two minutes past seven—Merren knew because she'd been checking her watch every thirty seconds since ten to seven—and brought wine, plus flowers for her and Carol, sweets for Queenie and Kitty, and, making Merren inwardly laugh, a teething ring for baby Samuel. The baby already had a couple of them, but they invariably went missing.

'Clever,' Merren murmured, her blue eyes alight with laughter that plainly Jarad had decided that if he was going to have to take his turn in nursing the fretful baby he obviously intended to give him something to chew on.

'My mother rang,' he answered, his glance on her laughing eyes. 'She suggested I found a pharmacy.'

'You told her you were coming to dinner—that Samuel...?'

'She was enraptured.'

'Oh, Jarad, she's going to be so disappointed.'

'You're too sensitive.' He smiled down at her—and then was annexed by Queenie and Kitty, and that was the end of any chance of private conversation for quite some while.

Carol had prepared melon wedges as a starter, and gave Kitty a threatening glance when she took a piece out of her mouth with her fingers and appeared about to complain that she didn't like it.

Remembering the way conversation had buzzed around the Montgomery dinner table, Merren was heartened that there were no dreadful silences at the Shepherd dinner table. In fact, everyone seemed on their best behavior, the conversation pleasant and varied.

But that was through the first course. She and Carol cleared away plates and retired to the kitchen to attend to the pasta, the sauce and the salad, and returned to have Queenie protest, 'I don't like pasta,' when her mother served her a portion.

'Nor do I,' Lewis Shepherd declared.

Merren's eyes went to Jarad, who was paying silent regard to everything. She felt embarrassed—but loyal. 'How about you?' she asked.

'My favourite meal,' he responded, as quick as a flash—just as if he wouldn't dare say anything else—and she laughed inwardly, and loved him the more for making such short work of her embarrassment.

But the rot had started to set in, and after Kitty reminded Queenie, 'Mummy said one squeak out of us and we're in trouble,' the ensuing squabble between the two girls was not conducive to maintaining an appetite.

'Stop that!' Carol ordered, with a sideways glance to her husband, who appeared not to notice his daughter's misbehaviour. 'Eat your meal and be grateful.'

'But…'

Merren thought it was time her guest's attention was taken away from the children. 'Your great-aunt is a very sprightly lady,' she addressed Jarad directly.

Grey eyes met deeply troubled blue ones. He smiled—and the baby decided to howl. 'Oh, G…' her father began, then caught Carol's hostile glance that clearly stated she would prefer that he didn't blaspheme in front of her daughters—and Carol went to attend to her son.

As soon as their mother had left the table, the girls began to squabble again. 'Do behave,' Robert said ineffectually.

And as they continued to squabble, and the baby continued to yell, Merren's father looked at his watch and invented a non-existent appointment. 'If you'll excuse me?' he smiled charmingly to their guest, and, pausing only to put his napkin down, he went out.

Robert looking longingly after him, every bit as if he wouldn't mind at all joining him at The Bull for a pie and a pint. But just then a tearful-looking Carol appeared, carrying a still crying baby, and presented him with his son before disappearing upstairs.

Robert looked at Merren. She ignored him and concentrated on sorting her nieces out. 'Eat what you can,' she instructed them, and bribery the name of the game—'I'll make you a banana split for pudding.' But still the baby cried.

Fifteen minutes later, Merren could only admire Jarad's tenacity in that he was still there. She would have thought that, like her father, he would have done a disappearing act long before this.

But there he was eating, watching, observing—any attempt at polite conversation had been done away with when, at the first sound of any voice but his own, baby Samuel had started off again.

Merren, rejecting Jarad's offer of help, cleared the table and brought out fruit salad for the grown-ups and hastily put together banana splits for the children, and took charge of the baby while her brother disposed of his desert.

The banana splits silenced her nieces for about three minutes before they started on at each other again—and Merren felt like doing the disappearing act herself. But, though she hadn't been serious, she had invited Jarad to dinner, so had to stick it out.

'Robert!' She attracted his attention over the din when it was obvious he wasn't going to attempt to exercise parental control over his daughters. He looked enquiringly over to her. Merren, aware that a defeated Carol had probably gone to lie down in the hope of renewing her batteries, took charge. 'You still have my car keys from this afternoon, so why not take Queenie and Kitty down to the brook. They can play Pooh Sticks for half an hour, or…'

'Oh, yes, Daddy!'

'You'll look after Sammie?'

The baby in her arms grizzled away, but he was much quieter when her brother and his two daughters had gone. Merren took a glance at Jarad—she wished she knew what he was thinking. Although, bearing in mind that the fracas that had passed for a mealtime, perhaps she didn't.

'You can drive off too, if you like,' she offered stiffly. 'You don't have to stay.'

He looked at her gravely. She felt dreadful; she wished he would smile. 'Is it always like this?' he asked quietly.

'Would you like some more fruit salad?' she replied.

And felt her heart lift when, his expression lightened, he asked gently, 'Did anyone ever tell you that you're pretty wonderful?'

Steady, Merren! One minute she'd been close to tears herself. Now she felt like beaming at him. 'I'm hearing it all the time,' she answered.

He smiled, and asked, 'Where's your dishwasher?'

'You're looking at it.'

Jarad's look was quiet upon her. 'Come and talk to me in the kitchen,' he said.

'You're not happy here?' After spending an hour of purgatory with her combative family at the dining table she expected him to be euphoric? The baby wasn't happy, at any rate, and started exercising his lungs again.

'Are all children like that?' Jarad wanted to know as Merren left her chair and began walking the floor with the wailing infant.

'Putting you off fatherhood?' she enquired sweetly, but answered, 'Some, I believe are as good as gold. This one—' she rocked the baby as she walked '—has, according to Carol, been a little demon from day one.' Jarad took that on board, then got to his feet and began to clear the table. 'I'll do that!' she objected.

'From where I'm standing, you appear to have your hands full,' he replied easily, and disappeared into the chaotic kitchen with his first cargo. Merren followed him. 'Do you have this load every night?' he asked, looking slightly winded at the debris created by feeding seven mouths.

'You can't make an omelette without breaking eggs,' she trotted out—and got the shock of her life when, having found somewhere to put down the used dishes he'd been holding, Jarad came over to her and, looking down into her slightly upturned face, bent and gently kissed her.

Her heart went off with a wild beat of its own, but as she stared speechlessly at Jarad, her brain having seized up, she suddenly became aware that the baby had stopped crying. Shaken—Samuel never stopped crying—well, it seemed that way—she took her gaze away from Jarad to look at the baby in her arms. He was looking up at Jarad—and was actually gummily grinning.

Still not believing it, she looked back at Jarad. 'Do that again,' she said, more as a joke than anything.

But Jarad, never one to refuse one of her invitations, it seemed, gathered her and the baby lightly in his arms. 'Any time,' he accepted, and, while her look was still telling him it was meant to be a joke, he bent and lingeringly touched his mouth to hers.

Then, while her insides were a veritable nonsense, Jarad broke his kiss and, his arms dropping from her, looked from her to the still grinning baby. On her part, Merren was stunned. She had been kissed before, and with more passion, but never had any kiss seemed more beautiful.

Feeling powerless to speak, to break that magic moment, she could only be grateful when Jarad, in no way similarly affected, took another step away and offered lightly, 'Just give me a ring if he starts making his presence known again in the middle of the night and I'll come over and "do that again".' Merren just had to laugh— was he wonderful or was he *wonderful*? She wasn't laughing a moment later, though, when he commented, rolling his sleeves up and heading for the sink, 'This isn't getting the washing-up done.'

He intended to tackle that mountain of washing-up? 'No!' she objected.

He turned. 'No?'

'I'll do it—when you've gone.'

She had Humphrey Bogart on her hands. 'You can't get rid of me that easy, sweetheart!' he told her with a tight top lip.

Oh, how she loved him! 'It's not right! You're a guest.'

'And you've done enough,' he stated firmly, and, with his glance on the wide-eyed child in her arms, 'And are still doing it. Take a seat and watch a novice at work. You're permitted to laugh if you absolutely have to.'

Since she was nursing the baby there was little she could do to prevent Jarad taking over her kitchen duties. And after a while Merren began to find it quite therapeutic, watching the inexpert but thorough way he went about cleaning dishes. And the baby stayed quiet! She could not help but wonder if perhaps the general strife that went on daily in the house had an adverse effect on the little chap. He had certainly shown a more cheerful side to his nature just now, when strife was absent—but what did she know?

'So tell me, Merren Shepherd.' Jarad dried his hands and, rolling down his sleeves, came and took a seat by her and the by now sleeping baby. 'What gives with this boyfriend of yours?'

Boyfriend! 'Gives?'

'Are you still virgin of this parish? You were working on it the last time we spoke on the subject?'

The cheek of it! She knew she had gone pink. 'And what gives in your non-celibate world?' Two could play at that game.

'For your information, I haven't had a date in weeks,' he answered—making her heart rejoice.

'You've been ill?' she questioned with mock concern. 'Just a minute!' she exclaimed. 'Isadora Thomas! You were out on a date a week last—Wednesday.'

'All right, Sherlock. I had a date ten days ago. You were out painting the town *last night*.'

Painting the town! He'd obviously never poked his nose round the door of that inauspicious watering hole The Bull. 'Guilty as charged,' she owned happily—wild horses wouldn't drag from her that Bertie Armstrong was just a jolly good pal, and didn't and never would come into the 'boyfriend' category.

For some silent moments Jarad studied her. But, when she'd expected some comment in connection with the subject they were discussing, he suddenly stretched up a hand to a wayward wisp of pale red hair and remarked softly, 'You look tired.'

As in—a wreck! 'What every girl wants to hear!'

'But beautiful!' He grinned to make it better. Though he was serious when he repeated his earlier question, 'Is it always like this here?'

Bedlam personified! 'Like what?' she queried innocently, knowing exactly what he meant.

'At a guess, I'd say you didn't know what hit you when your brother and his family moved in—followed by your father.'

What could she say? Nothing. Her loyalty to her family decreed she said not one word of the giant adjustment she'd had to make when her quiet solitude had first been shattered. Suddenly, though, Jarad was dipping his hand inside his pocket and bringing out a key, and placing it on the kitchen table near to her.

'Keep that for a while,' he urged. 'I've a spare at

home. It's to the door of Birchwood, a house I inherited from my grandmother last year.' Merren stared at him, somewhat taken aback that he was giving her a key to keep for a while! But that was before he went on, 'I'd half thought I might drive down to stay overnight when I left here—it's in the New Forest—but I've gone off the idea. However, there's nothing to stop you going.'

'You're offering me the loan of the house?' she questioned, her eyes widening.

'If you feel like a break—if things get a little too much for you here. You could go next weekend,' he suggested.

He was offering her the use of Birchwood, his New Forest house! 'Oh, I couldn't!' she protested.

'Of course you could,' he asserted. And added, for undermining good measure, 'Think of it, Merren, peace and quiet—and a lovely big double bed to sleep in.'

'Oh, don't!' It sounded bliss—pure bliss—pure and *utter* bliss. 'You won't be there?' she found herself asking—as if it mattered. She wasn't going.

'You'll be all by yourself. There's a pantry loaded with tinned and bottled foodstuffs.'

But Merren shook her head. Had to before she started thinking in terms of what a splendid chance it would be for her to catch up on her sleep and to renew *her* batteries. 'Thanks all the same. It's more than generous of you. But…'

'Keep the key anyway, in case you change your mind. It's still got the address label on it which my mother attached while waiting to pass it over to me.'

Merren went to say no again, but then heard the sound of the doors on her car being crashed shut. Her brother and her nieces had been out longer than expected, but were now back. She'd have to see Queenie and Kitty to bed straight away or Carol would be upset again.

The outer door to the kitchen was jerked half off its hinges as Queenie, with Kitty at her heels, stampeded in, startling the baby awake. It was the cue for his rosebud mouth to open, that pretty little mouth instantly changing to a gaping hole as he started to holler. Peace had ended.

Jarad stood up, took hold of the key, and pressed it into her hands. 'Think about it, Merren: silence, tranquillity.'

'Don't be mean!' she laughed. And as he took out his car keys and it became obvious he wasn't delaying his departure now they'd been invaded, she asked sweetly, 'Not stopping for coffee?'

'Love you,' he grinned. She wished he did.

CHAPTER SIX

MERREN felt unsettled after Jarad had left on Saturday. It was a feeling that stayed with her through the following week. If the phone rang, though it rarely did, her adrenalin would start to pump. It might be him. It never was. And why would he ring anyway? Well—he might, if his mother...

He might call round too. If his mother was giving him a sort of third degree on how things were faring between them—he might call round.

But he neither called round nor phoned, and Merren was feeling all over the place emotionally. Her father was getting short-tempered about just about everything, and her nieces were more unruly than ever, and Carol wasn't getting any better, and Robert was doing little to help.

A row flared up between her brother and sister-in-law on Friday night, and Merren, without a room to go to, wished herself miles away. As Carol detailed a long list of her brother's shortcomings, so Merren went out into the garden. She could always take up Jarad's New Forest offer, she supposed, as she surveyed the sorry state of the rear garden her mother had so loved. Flowers and shrubs broken, the lawn moth-eaten and dug up in places—but children had to play somewhere.

Merren knew she wouldn't be going to Birchwood, the house Jarad's grandmother had left him, but that didn't stop the idea from having tremendous appeal. Merren went back indoors. The row between Carol and Robert was over, but the tension was palpable.

She found herself thinking that Carol didn't get out enough, and on impulse asked, 'Fancy coming for a walk, Carol? We could…' But Carol was already shaking her head.

'No, thanks,' she refused bleakly as Queenie and Kitty—sent to bed for some misdemeanour—started shrieking in argument overhead.

'You can take the girls if you like,' Robert suggested.

And was soundly rounded on by his wife for his trouble. 'That's right. As always, try to get out of your responsibilities. You'd do nothing if…'

At that point Merren took herself off for a walk. She longed for the days of peace and quiet, and felt mean that she should do so. But she didn't feel built for this strife, this constant strife. She didn't need it, didn't want it— but they were her family.

She was supposed to be meeting Bertie and the gang at The Bull later—she couldn't face it. No more than she could face going home yet. She found herself walking by the bridge where she had suggested Robert and the girls played Pooh Sticks last Saturday. She went and leaned over to watch the water in the brook below.

She reflected sadly on how Robert and Carol were not getting along too well just now. It was a difficult time for Robert, but difficult for Carol too. She had accused him of always trying to get out of his responsibilities— was that true?

Merren had an uncomfortable feeling that it was. And suddenly she had an even more uncomfortable feeling that she was partly to blame. Many were the occasions when she'd taken the girls for a walk, for a drive, or dropped one or other of them—or both—off somewhere, while their father stayed home doing what? Very little, really.

All at once her thoughts were going up a previously uncharted channel. Would Robert do more, cohere more with Carol if she wasn't around? Would Robert perhaps buck his ideas up, do more for Carol and his offspring, if she wasn't around so much?

She'd been away overnight only two weeks ago, Merren remembered, but hadn't noticed any difference in Carol and Robert's relationship when she'd returned. And, remembering the state her home had been in when she'd got back, Robert hadn't moved himself to do any tidying up in the short time she had been away.

Merren had another nightmare that night. She found it upsetting. It was the first one she'd had since she'd come back from Hillmount. She had begun to wonder, to hope, that by talking it all out of her system with Jarad's father, her nightmares were a thing of the past.

She was up early, but her quiet interlude was over when the rest of the family descended and the bickering started—her father being of no help at all. Merren took herself off to visit Uncle Amos, and began to think the unthinkable—she'd told Jarad that she couldn't make use of his New Forest house, but suddenly she began to wonder.

By the time she was driving back home she thought that perhaps she might. She opened the outer door to her home—and heard the free-for-all going on inside—and suddenly knew that she would. It mystified her how she and the rest of her family should share the same blood, yet, apart from about a five per cent similarity, be so otherwise totally different!

Once indoors, she packed a few necessities, and, when she could get a word in, announced she would be spending the night in Jarad's New Forest home.

Her father came out to her car with her. 'I'm a bit

short, Merren—I haven't even got the price of a pint. I don't suppose you could...' Merren handed over a precious ten-pound note.

Birchwood was a four-bedroomed house set in an isolated area, its closest neighbour down a lane and round a bend. There were beautiful trees and shrubs around, and from the immaculate garden—did some other 'old retainer' keep it so, perhaps?—there was not another house to be seen.

Merren found homes for the few provisions she had brought with her, and at once began to feel at ease in Jarad's inherited property. She felt relaxed and comfortable. Maybe she had needed to get away.

An hour later and she began to feel even more settled. The house was kept well aired, she discovered, so someone—probably yet another 'retainer'—must come here once a week and check the house over.

Another hour went by, and Merren was starting to feel as if she were a totally different person, only then able to acknowledge that at home she had begun to feel as strung up as her sister-in-law. Perhaps she should move out. Perhaps there was a way...

It had been a lovely summer's day, and late that afternoon Merren found a canvas chair and, relaxing more and more by the second, went and sat outside. She stayed there until early evening, but, with only herself to think of, decided she could have her dinner at any old time. She wasn't hungry.

She closed her eyes. Jarad, oh, thank you, Jarad. Thank you a million times. Th... She heard a sound. In her tranquil haven she heard a sound that was suspiciously like the purr of a car's engine. She opened her eyes— and then her eyes shot wide! *Jarad!*

Her adrenalin started pumping wildly as Jarad steered

his Jaguar on to the standing area in front of the double garage. He looked across and waved—she couldn't tell if he was surprised to see her, but he couldn't be half as surprised as she was to see him!

It was no good wondering what he was doing here. He owned the place! She, Merren began to quickly realise, would have to go. She should, she supposed belatedly, have phoned him to tell him she intended to take him up on his offer to stay at Birchwood this weekend—then he would have been able to tell her that he intended to use it himself this weekend. No matter. Even knowing that she would shortly be on her way, it was just wonderful, quite, quite wonderful, to see him so unexpectedly.

She was out of her chair by the time he was coming over. 'I should have phoned!' she blurted out. 'I should have let you know I intended using that key—only...only I didn't know myself until this morning that I...'

'Good evening, Merren. How are you?' he butted into her gabbled apology.

What could she do? She loved him. She laughed. 'I'll leave,' she sobered to tell him. 'I'll just get my things together and...'

'I wouldn't hear of it!' Jarad interrupted firmly, his glance smiling into her deeply blue eyes.

'But you...' she protested, feeling quite terrible that Jarad had arrived expecting to have his house to himself, only to find her there.

'The house is big enough for the two of us,' he cut in again.

Merren stared at him in wonder, her heart going nineteen to the dozen again. Was he saying that they could stay there together? That she needn't sit and think of him without any idea of when she would see him again—if ever? That she could spend the evening and perhaps some of the next morning in his company?

'You w-want to spend some time alone in the country,' she felt honour bound to insist—while at the same time wanting to consign her conscience to the nearest bin.

'You don't want me here?'

She stared at him, too startled to be anything other than honest. 'It's not that!'

'You'd prefer I went to a hotel?'

'Jarad!' she wailed.

'Merren,' he said pleasantly.

'I'll leave!' she said crisply.

'Isn't that where I came in?'

'There isn't a hotel around here that I noticed. Besides...'

'You'd have me return to London—oh, heartless creature!'

She was starting to feel more relaxed again. Whether she left or Jarad did—though of course she'd have to be the one to go—it was unbelievably fantastic just to be with him. 'What's the matter with London?' she paused in her argument to enquire.

'My mother's there.'

Merren had earlier realised that Jarad's parents lived only about twenty minutes from his New Forest house—but apparently his mother wasn't there this weekend. 'Your mother's staying in your home this weekend?' she asked.

'With Aunt Rosa. My father's at a conference in Sweden. My mother decided to stay behind and take in a show she wanted to see.'

'Doesn't she mind you coming away and leaving her...?'

'Are you going to make me a cup of coffee?'

'Come in.' She invited him into his house, and they were both in the kitchen before he answered her question.

'My mother has the impression I'm busy somewhere with you.'

'Oh, Jarad, you didn't tell her...?' She broke off, capitulating. 'I'm sorry. It's what we agreed, wasn't it?'

'Put your honest soul away,' he bade her pleasantly. 'I didn't have to say anything in particular—just see to it that both my mother and my aunt were catered for and say I had plans.'

'Ah!' Merren used her brain.

'What does "ah" mean?'

She stared at him, an imp of mischief dancing in her eyes. 'Just that I can see it would rather cramp your style to bring someone "back for coffee" with your mother there.'

'For that, you can cook dinner,' Jarad announced. Though his tone was serious when he added, 'I refuse to let you pack up and go, Merren—do I have your permission to bring my gear in?'

Bliss, perfect bliss. 'Oh, all right,' she said begrudgingly, the smile that followed belying her tone.

Dinner was a mixed affair of the food she and Jarad had brought. Since he had brought a cardboard box loaded to the brim, not to mention the plentiful supply in the pantry, she could see they wouldn't starve if they stayed there for a week. If only!

After dinner, and having attended to their used dishes and tidied up, they went for a walk. They walked and talked, and at one stage Jarad even placed an arm about her shoulders. He took it away again after about a minute, but Merren had never felt so happy. Her thoughts were only for him, and she didn't care if she was being selfish. She didn't want to think of her family, or the trauma that went with being part of a family that seemed to live in constant strife.

It was starting to get dark when they got back to the house, and as they went inside Merren suddenly began to get nervous that, having been in such perfect harmony with Jarad, he might catch a glimpse of how utterly in love with him she was. She couldn't have that.

'I think I'll go up to bed,' she announced shortly—and could have cringed when Jarad looked a mite surprised.

'What did I do?' he asked, his mouth picking up good-humouredly at the corners.

'Sorry—did you want me to make you a drink or something?'

'That's what I like—a willing slave!'

'So make your own nightcap,' she laughed, and explained, weak though she considered the explanation to be, 'I've been longing to get into that bed ever since I took the sheets out of the airing cupboard to make it.'

Apparently her explanation was plausible. 'Poor little Merren,' Jarad murmured, coming over to her.

'Don't you dare feel sorry for me!' she erupted, but laughed when he did.

'Who would have that much nerve?' he teased, of her fierceness.

'Goodnight.' She smiled—and felt as if her heart might leap out of her body when unhurriedly Jarad gathered her into his arms.

'Goodnight,' he answered softly, and gently kissed her.

Merren floated up the stairs. She was showered, night-dress-clad and in bed before she came anywhere near to coming down to earth. It had been nothing short of enchanting to be in Jarad's arms. His kiss magical.

She was still awake when an hour or so later she heard him coming up the stairs. An hour after that and she was still wide awake. She didn't want to go to sleep. She wanted to savour every moment of being with him, just her and him under the same roof. She could sleep any old time. For now it was just her and Jarad, and he was gentle and funny, sophisticated yet kind—and she loved him.

She was glad that because Mrs Montgomery and her sister were using his London home as a base that weekend they had given Jarad cause to move out. And suddenly it dawned on Merren that, had he had a date arranged for that evening which he didn't—in the circumstances—want his mother to know about, he could easily have spent the weekend in some London hotel.

Merren closed her eyes as sleep came to claim her, a sweet smile on her mouth. Jarad, all too wonderfully, couldn't have arranged to see any of his Isadora-Thomas-type 'friends' that weekend. He had, instead, come down here.

Merren slept dreamlessly. She was still asleep when someone knocking at her door brought her to the surface. 'Come in,' she called sleepily, and struggled to sit up while at the same time endeavouring to hide her delight when, bearing a cup and saucer on a tray, Jarad, dressed casually, entered her room.

'Tea, madam,' he greeted her.

'Oh, Jarad!' she exclaimed, coming rapidly awake. 'You're spoiling me.'

'It's about time somebody did,' he answered lightly, bending to place the tea down on her bedside table.

Merren looked up at him, and away. He was closer than she had thought. 'Er—talking of time—what time is it?' she asked.

'Coming up to eight o'clock.'

'It isn't!' As if not trusting him, she stretched out a

hand to the table for her watch. He wasn't lying, she saw. 'I never sleep this late!' she exclaimed, watching as he came and sat down on the side of her bed.

'With Master Samuel exercising his lung power so vigorously, I'd be surprised if you did,' he answered, and seemed amused; he was in good humour anyway, Merren noted.

But this was all too splendid, and, reluctant though she was to end it, she knew it couldn't go on. 'Thank you for the tea,' she said primly, suddenly conscious that her hair must be all over the place and that she hadn't got a scrap of make-up on, and, belatedly, that she must have frequently moved in the night because her nightdress was all twisted out of alignment. She went to straighten it, and felt her skin tingle all over when, his fingers touching her shoulder, Jarad matter-of-factly tugged the strap of her nightdress into place. She pulled the sheet up to her chin, hiding her curves and then, since he seemed in no hurry to leave her room, she announced from her bed, 'I'll just drink this and think about making tracks back to Surrey.'

'You can't go back yet!' Jarad objected, warming her to the depths of her being.

'Why can't I?' she argued—well, it wouldn't do if she threw her arms around his neck in instant eager and grateful submission, would it?

'Heartless woman—who's going to cook my lunch?' he demanded.

It wasn't the best offer she'd ever had, but it would do. She supposed she should demur, say that she had to get back to the family, but Jarad might say, Fine. Bye, and, having the chance to spend a few more hours with him dangled in front of her, she just couldn't miss this chance.

'Oh, all right,' she grumbled, and he laughed, and her heart rejoiced.

'How did you sleep?' he asked, and Merren, recalling how she had disturbed him—albeit that he had been awake reading—the last time they had spent the night under the same roof, knew he was asking if she'd had a nightmare last night.

'I slept like the proverbial log,' she was pleased to be able to tell him.

His eyes went from her smiling eyes down to her sweetly curving mouth, and abruptly he stood up. He was on his way to the door when he commented, 'Good— you'll be fit for a nice long walk after breakfast.'

Joy didn't begin to cover her inner feelings when later she and Jarad tramped lanes and fields, stopping every now and then to look, to admire, to breathe the air. Sometimes they talked—on any subject that came up— while at others they walked in companionable silence. And all the while Merren stored up memories for when this golden time was over.

All of this would never have taken place had she not been mugged and subsequently borrowed money from him. But, while she still had every intention of paying him back every penny of that money, she wanted for the moment to forget all about it. To just enjoy the bonus of it all—the bonus of being with him.

They passed a village shop on the way back, and stopped to pick up some Sunday newspapers. But back at the house, when Merren was thinking of making a start on getting the lunch together, she heard a car pull on to the parking area. Both their cars were garaged, so as far as their caller knew there was no one at home.

Jarad took a look out of the window, then looked back at Merren. 'I'll give you three guesses,' he offered.

She stared at him. 'Give me a clue.'

'A female of the species who, many moons ago, lived here with her mother. A female whom I suspect still has a key—and has called to check the place over in my absence.'

'Your mother!' Merren guessed, and, in a sudden panic, 'She'll think we're lovers!' she squeaked.

'You could be right,' he agreed, and decided, 'I'll come clean—I'll tell her the truth.'

Not while she still owed him, he wouldn't. 'Don't you dare!'

'You don't want me to?' he asked in surprise.

Merren shook her head. That money she owed was starting to be a lead weight around her neck! 'Just make sure your mother checks the upstairs rooms and sees that two of the bedrooms are occupied.' She didn't think it at all funny when he laughed.

'You're cute,' he informed her, teasing when she was feeling suddenly uptight and didn't want him to be teasing. 'You don't think my mother might not conclude from the evidence that you snore and I slept alone—er—afterwards?'

Merren, feeling confused that, while still loving him, she could at one and the same time hate him, knew she had gone pink and didn't deign to answer. And before Mrs Montgomery could let herself in Jarad went to the front door. Merren heard Mrs Montgomery exclaim in surprise, heard Jarad answer, and had but a few seconds to get on top of her agitation before he was ushering their visitor in.

'Look who's just arrived,' he announced pleasantly, but as Merren, ignoring him, went forward, Mrs Montgomery broke into an apologetic speech.

'I'm so sorry. I didn't mean to... I've just dropped

Jarad's aunt Rosa off—she lives not far away—and I thought, while I was so close, I'd come and check...' She broke off. While clearly pleased at evidence that her son was most definitely going 'steady' with Merren, at the same time she was obviously feeling very awkward to have intruded.

Merren liked her, and in her empathy for Mrs Montgomery's discomfiture forgot her own embarrassment and smiled. 'We were just discussing lunch. I'd love it if you would join us?' A flicked glance to Jarad showed from his raised eyebrows that he hadn't expected that—serve him right.

But his mother was already declining. 'Oh, no, thank you very much, Merren. I've people coming to tea and must get back—this was only meant to be a flying visit.'

Jarad recovered sufficiently to insist his mother share a cup of coffee with them, but she stayed only a short while and they went out to wave her off. Merren had conversed comfortably with Mrs Montgomery while she had been there, but unspeaking was how Merren returned indoors with Jarad.

Somehow, some of the magic of the day seemed to have disappeared, and now she was the one who felt awkward. She heard Jarad come into the kitchen behind her, but felt she had nothing she wanted to say to him. Her voice seemed stuck somehow, down in her throat.

He, however, was having no such problem. 'You hate me, don't you?' He addressed her back, his tone even, giving her a very clear indication that he cared not one whit either way. If she loved him or hated him, it was all the same to him.

She turned about, keeping her eyes lowered so he couldn't see her pain at his total indifference. 'I'll go and get my bag and leave you in peace,' she stated quietly, and was almost past him when he snaked out a hand and brought her to face him. She wanted to go, but he held her firm. She wouldn't look at him.

At least, she'd had no intention of looking at him. But that was before he raised his objection to her leaving by asking aggrievedly, 'What about my lunch?'

Her head shot up, and she stared at him. Then he grinned—and she folded. 'Pig!' she becalled him, sunshine entering her heart, that magic back—did being in love make you temperamental? It would seem so.

'Still hate me?' he wanted to know.

Inside she was laughing. 'Not enough to deprive you of your lunch.'

'That's good,' he replied. 'I don't hate you.'

'You don't?'

'Who could? You're lovely to a chap's mother.'

Oh, she loved him. 'Where's your potato peeler?' she demanded bossily, just to let him know his charm, his wonderful charm, affected her not in the slightest.

'You're looking at it.' It was their joke; she laughed. Jarad stared down at her upturned mouth. 'Are you going to give me a kiss so I'll know you forgive me—for whatever it was I did?'

'Brace yourself,' she said, and stretched up and kissed him—and wanted to go on kissing him—especially when she felt his arms come about her. But this would never do. 'Don't make a meal of it, Montgomery,' she told him coolly. 'You'll spoil your lunch.'

He let her go—she wished he hadn't. And he, muttering something about 'potato peeler', went to look in a drawer to see if they had one.

Steak, potatoes and broccoli, with fresh fruit to follow, seemed the finest meal she had ever eaten. Soon, she knew, she must end this tremendous time. Soon she would have to make noises about leaving—but not yet.

She took up a Sunday paper to read; Jarad took another. She read some of hers, but, since she'd schooled herself not to look over at him every two seconds, she had no idea how much he was reading.

It was around a quarter to four when she knew she could delay her departure no longer. She put down the newspaper she wasn't really reading and addressed the one Jarad held in front of him. 'I'll make a pot of tea, then I'll get off,' she said brightly.

Slowly, he lowered his paper. 'Do you have to?'

Her heart lifted—he was asking her to stay a while longer? Common sense arrived. Don't be absurd. 'You'd prefer coffee?'

'Why not stay another night? You could drive to your office from here in the morning.'

Oh, it was tempting! Perhaps Jarad wouldn't leave until later this evening—she'd have the chance of a few more hours in his company. 'I told my family I'd be back tonight.'

'Well, I know they've got a phone,' he replied. 'Think of it, Merren, another night in that bed.'

'You're being unfair!' she protested, weakening by the second.

He smiled that smile that turned her backbone to water. 'Will you dial the number or shall I?'

She smiled back. How could she not? 'I'll get you something to eat before you leave,' she replied, accepting his suggestion to stay.

'I couldn't let you,' he answered.

She'd not long ago cooked lunch! 'Suddenly you're getting scruples about me labouring over a hot stove! Why not?'

'Because, sweet Merren, I have to be off early, and, as lovely as you are, as little beauty sleep as you need, I wouldn't dream of allowing you to get up with the dawn to make breakfast for me.'

She stared at him, more pleasure washing over her. How she didn't break out into one heartfelt joyous grin as what he was saying started to penetrate, she couldn't have said. 'You're staying overnight too?' she queried, staggered that her tone should sound so matter-of-fact when she was jumping for joy inside.

But he was serious. 'You don't mind?' he asked, and Merren knew then she had only to say the word and he would be gone—but she wasn't having that.

'Of course not,' she answered stoutly. 'It's your house,' she added—to let him know 'personal' didn't come into it.

But it *was* personal, to her. She savoured every moment of the hours that followed. Just to sit with him, to talk with him, to eat with him had her inner happiness overflowing. When, however, she found herself again laughing at some witticism he'd made, Merren started to fear she was in danger of giving away how wonderful she felt just to be with him.

True, Jarad appeared to be enjoying her company too, but that could be all part and parcel of his natural charm. And in any event, while he might find her company quite pleasant, it was nowhere near being in love with her. On what she knew of him so far he would run a mile at the very idea.

When she found she was again laughing at something he'd said, Merren decided, reluctantly, that she had better get out of there. She glanced at her watch, glad to see that it was ten o'clock. 'I think I'll leave you to it,' she remarked, getting to her feet.

'You're going to bed?' Jarad was on his feet too.

'I have to go home to change before I go to the office—I'll have to be up early too,' she explained, feeling more than able to sit up talking with him all night and still be fit enough to do a whole day's work tomorrow.

Jarad looked at her. 'Never change,' he said after a moment. 'You're unique as you are.'

She felt this was a compliment, but also suddenly felt unaccountably shy. 'I'm not sure how I'm supposed to take that,' she grinned, and to show that she wasn't in the least shy—perish the thought—she went over to him and stretched up and kissed him on the cheek. 'Goodnight,' she said, and would have turned away, but Jarad caught a hold of her.

And suddenly her heartbeats were going wild, because Jarad had gathered her in his arms, and, forget any other kisses they had shared, he placed his mouth over hers in an all-male, seeking, giving kiss that left her breathless.

When he let go his hold on her, Merren took a staggered step backwards and stared at him. 'Wh-what was that for?' she gasped.

'Treating me like an uncle,' he answered honestly.

Merren went to bed laughing—she had kissed him on the cheek and he hadn't liked it. She showered and got into bed, reflecting that he had kissed her—a proper man-to-woman kiss this time—and she had loved it.

Her bed was delicious. She stretched out in it, reflecting on her day, on yesterday, on this wonderful time she had spent with Jarad—doing nothing in particular but walking, talking, laughing, eating. He had kissed her, though he'd meant nothing by it—but it was another memory to add to her store.

She again slept dreamlessly, but awakened to find it was daylight—and that Jarad was in her room! Merren was instantly wide awake, and saw from his still slightly damp hair that he was freshly showered and shaved. He was robe-clad, and if the tray in his hand bearing a cup and saucer was anything to go by he was bringing her early-morning tea.

'I did knock,' he excused, coming over to her bedside table and placing the tray down.

'What time is it?' she asked, sitting up.

'Five-thirty,' he answered, looking down at her from his lofty height. 'I'll say cheerio now, and leave you to lock up,' he stated easily, and Merren started to come rapidly awake to the fact that once he'd thrown some clothes on he would be off, and she had no idea when— if ever—she would see him again.

Already he was bending as if to make his farewells. Her skin felt scorched when he lightly caught hold of her uncovered shoulders, and just as lightly touched his lips to her cheek.

'Be good,' he bade her, and went to straighten up— only she wasn't having that. She caught hold of him by his towelling robe.

He halted, his eyes questioning what that was about, and Merren grinned up at him. 'When did I become your aunt?' she questioned impishly, and while he looked at her, as if to say, This isn't a very good idea, she tightened her grip on his robe—and pulled him nearer.

Near enough for her to stretch up and kiss him anyway. She knew that by comparison she must be a novice in the kissing stakes. But she did her best to return the compliment of the thorough job he had made of kissing her last night.

'T-take that!' she exclaimed feebly as their kiss ended. But she didn't want to let go of him. In fact, she felt incapable of letting him go. As he stared down at her, as if slightly winded, she still had hold of his robe. And, simply because she couldn't help it, she kissed him again.

She never afterwards knew whether she'd meant it to be a brief touch to his mouth—a kiss goodbye—but suddenly Jarad was taking over and she was more being kissed than kissing. Jarad was close up to her, sitting, half leaning on her bed, and she wasn't holding his robe, she was being held, and it wasn't stopping at just one kiss, and it was all too wonderful.

'Merren.' He said her name, and she wanted to get closer to him.

'Jarad,' she whispered, and had her wish to be closer when his arms came all the way around her and he gathered her to him.

Her arms went around him and she rejoiced in their closeness as kiss after marvellous kiss they shared. He pushed the strap of her nightdress aside and kissed her shoulder, and suddenly a fire was igniting inside her.

She wasn't sure that she didn't say his name again, but knew only rapture when he moved her to lie down, and then came to lie down beside her. With her heart racing madly she looked at him, and kissed him, experiencing passion such as she had never known when he placed his seeking lips over her slightly parted mouth.

Merren closed her eyes in rapture at his touch as Jarad, the man she loved, gently caressed her back, his hands moving unhurriedly to the front of her. She clutched on to him when those wonderful caressing hands captured the swollen globes of her breasts.

'Jarad!' She did cry his name, but it was a cry of wanting.

'Sweet, sweet, Merren,' he breathed, and seemed to know what her cry had been all about. For he kissed her again, and somehow, while she was too taken up with the emotions that were rioting within her to know exactly how, he relieved her body of its covering.

Indeed, she only became aware that she was naked when she realised that, though Jarad had removed his robe, there was only the one undergarment he had bothered to put on between them. She had no idea when or where the bedclothes had disappeared.

She swallowed hard as he held her to him, and she felt her bare breasts against his naked chest. She wanted to tell him that she loved him, and knew a moment of confusion because she felt too shy to tell him that while she was glorying unashamed in the feel of her naked body against him. She felt the warmth of his touch caress and mould her uncovered breasts, and smiled shyly when he stared down into her deeply blue eyes.

'You're beautiful,' he murmured, and lowered his head to her breasts, and made a total nonsense of her when, taking one of her breasts to his mouth, he moulded it, and tantalised the hardened pink tip with his tongue.

'Jarad!' She called his name in an ecstasy of wanting.

He raised his head. 'Are you all right?' he asked, his voice thickened with desire.

'Oh, yes, yes. I want you,' she murmured shyly. 'I want you so much.'

'Sweet love,' he breathed, and gently kissed her again.

Merren kissed him back, a mutual fire of wanting burning between them. She wanted to touch him, and as their legs entwined, and she pressed herself instinctively closer to him, and rejoiced in the groan of pure need that escaped him, she stroked her hands gloriously over his hair-roughened chest, and kissed his nipples.

Then she was in his ardent embrace again, and Jarad was holding her close up against him, his hands on her pert behind, inviting her closer, yet closer to him.

She kissed him, wanting him, wanting him—oh, so much. But as his touch became even more intimate, his moving fingers caressing over her belly and thighs while her body screamed out her need for him—she suddenly, abruptly and confusingly, started to panic.

'No!' she said on a sob of a breath, when what she meant was, Yes, oh, yes, please—*now*!

Jarad stilled. 'No?' he questioned hoarsely.

But her tongue denied her. Even when Jarad looked at her incredulously, and she knew he would be furious with her, she was still denying the needs of her own body, her need for him. 'I'm—s-sorry,' she choked huskily.

'You're—*sorry*?'

He still wasn't believing it, she could tell—and could hardly blame him. She doubted that any woman had ever let their lovemaking get this far and then, in bed, naked, had told him no. But something, something deep inside of her, seemed to be ruling.

She moved from him. He seemed stunned—and let her go. Merren sat up and presented him with her back. 'I... You...' She had no excuses. All she knew was that she wanted to—but couldn't. 'I...' She wanted to tell him she loved him, but knew in advance that that wouldn't make anything better. 'Y-you're—going to be late,' she said jerkily. 'You s-said you had to be off early.'

Merren wished she hadn't turned her back on him, wished that she could see his face. Though she guessed she wouldn't see anything she wanted to see in his gaze—not now. She knew without doubt that she was at this moment his very least favourite person.

His voice, when it came, confirmed that. 'Next time,' he began coolly, getting up from the bed, 'I'll set my alarm for four o'clock.' And with that, he went.

Merren sat where she was for ages afterwards. She

heard various sounds, him moving around the house, heard him getting his car out of the garage, and heard him driving away. She felt suddenly cold and weepy, and quite bereft, because she knew then, if she knew nothing else, that he would never be setting his alarm for four o'clock so that they could make leisurely love before he went off early somewhere.

Because quite simply she wasn't going to get another chance to be so perfectly as one with him. She had ruined any hope of that. He wasn't the sort of man who would invite another helping of rejection. There would—she knew without the smallest doubt—be no next time. And it was all her fault.

CHAPTER SEVEN

HER family were up and about when Merren arrived at her home, but were uncommunicative at that hour, and she was glad about that—her head and heart were still too full for her to want any intrusion.

She was at work on time, but went through the routine of her job semi-automatically while at the same time she was still pondering why, when she loved Jarad so, and making love with him had seemed so right, she had, at the last moment, called a halt.

Oh, heavens, he must hate her—and it wasn't his hatred that she wanted.

She recalled thinking before something about being in love making you temperamental. Well, you couldn't get more temperamental in her book than giving off all the signs of being eager to be made love to—and then abruptly changing your mind.

Merren was driving herself home from work when it finally came to her why she had acted as she had. She owed Jarad money, and something perverse in her nature—call it pride, call it what you will—would not allow her to give herself to him; not when she owed him money.

She pulled her car on to the standing area and parked it behind her father's rattle-trap of a vehicle and, her thoughts still with Jarad and that money she owed him, knew she was somehow going to have to pay him back with all speed. That outstanding debt was spoiling everything—not that there was anything to spoil. Jarad had kissed her and...

Her eyes grew misty. She pulled herself together, and had a smile on her face when her two nieces came out to greet her.

Merren was not smiling later, however. They were all seated round the dinner table, baby Samuel appearing to have turned over a new leaf and having exchanged tears for grummy smiles, when Kitty remarked how good the fish fingers and mash were, and Queenie took up, 'Better than Saturday, when Mummy spoiled the dinner and Grandad swore and ordered a take-away, and—oh!' She broke off to gasp.

It was faintly possible, given she had her own thoughts to think about, that the eight-year-old's chatter might have gone over Merren's head. But that guilty sounding 'oh!', coupled with the fact that the other adults, including her sister-in-law, were giving Queenie most definite 'shut up' looks, made Merren go back over what her niece had just said. Suddenly she knew that something was very wrong here.

'Oh?' she queried quietly.

'I wasn't supposed to tell!' Queenie confessed with an apprehensive look at her mother. 'Grandad said it was his treat, but Kitty and me weren't to tell you because you'd missed a feast—we had *everything*—and you might not like it.'

Merren didn't like it. Not because she'd missed 'a feast' but because she knew quite well that the excuse— she might not like it—had only been invented to try and keep her nieces from telling about it. Anyone who knew her—and who knew her better than her family?—would know that it wouldn't matter a jot to her that they'd had a feast and she hadn't. But what concerned her more was that she knew for a fact that the only money her father had had on Saturday was the ten pounds she had given him. A feast for five, with *everything*, would have cost considerably more than ten pounds.

While Carol was instructing her daughters that they could leave the table and go outside to play if they didn't want anything else to eat—and they ran off—Merren looked at her father. She supposed her expression must have revealed that she was upset that he must have borrowed money from Uncle Amos—money Uncle Amos couldn't afford to lend—to pay for the feast of *'everything'*

Her father was belligerent in his defence, anyway, when he pre-empted the question of if he had borrowed money from his brother-in-law by declaring, 'He was happy to let me have the money.'

Of course he was; Uncle Amos would give his last penny away! But this wasn't good enough. Uncle Amos had the same outgoings as everyone else. 'When are you going to pay him back?' she asked forthrightly, feeling sick at heart that, before she could think of repaying Jarad the money she owed him, it looked as if she was going to have to clear her father's debt to her uncle first.

'I didn't think I'd have to pay him back,' her father had the unprincipled nerve to state. But then proceeded to send Merren spinning into shock when he went on cheerfully, 'I mean, you being his long-term girlfriend and everything.' While her eyes shot wide, he carried on, 'After all, he *has* taken you to meet his parents. You stayed with them the other weekend, and...'

'*Jarad!*' she gasped. 'Are you saying that *Jarad*...that *he* was the one who...?'

'Who else did you think I meant? You know as well

as me that he's loaded. And I know you've just spent the weekend with him. So...'

'How...?' Utterly staggered, Merren couldn't think straight.

Then her brother was chipping in. 'Don't make a fuss, Merren. We all know your boyfriend's more affluent than affluent. A couple of hundred isn't going to make the smallest difference to him.'

A couple of hundred! She was reeling. 'Did *you* borrow from him too?' she asked sharply.

'I didn't get the chance!' her brother complained. 'He'd been and gone by the time we came back on Saturday.'

Saturday! She couldn't take it in. Jarad had been *here*—last Saturday? He had called at her home before he'd come to Birchwood? Surely not! He couldn't have. Or, if he had, he'd had no idea that she'd be there.

Her brain wouldn't work. She tried to stick with fact rather than supposition. 'How much?' she turned to her father to ask. 'Just how much did you bor...take from him.'

'Four hundred,' her father returned promptly, with not so much as a blush about him.

'Four hundred!' she exclaimed, absolutely staggered.

But before she could ask him what on earth he wanted four hundred pounds for—though knowing her father there probably wouldn't have to be a reason—he was saying, 'He said not to mention to you that he'd called, but I can't see that it matters. Anyhow, four hundred was all he had on him.' *All!* Her father was just *too* much. 'But he said he'd be passing a cashpoint on his way, so he'd be able to get some more m...'

'On his way where?' Merren butted in, ice-cold fingers starting to clutch at her heart.

Her father shrugged. 'I'd already told him he'd missed you by a couple of hours, and that by now you'd probably arrived in the New Forest, and he...'

Jarad had known she'd be at Birchwood! Merren couldn't bear to hear any more. Without another word she left the room, picking up her bag and her car keys on her way out. She had no idea where she was going, but she couldn't bear to stay in the same room with the three of them another minute. Even Carol, by her silence, had condoned what had gone on—aside from the fact Carol would know her husband's father never had any money, she too had been giving Queenie 'shut up' looks about who had really paid for Saturday's dinner. It was intolerable! And Jarad had known...

Waving absently to her two nieces who, perhaps seeing her set expression, for once didn't ask to go with her, Merren got into her car and drove off. Her head was still in a whirl, but she needed to think. It was so important to her that she paid Jarad back the two thousand as quickly as she could—now here she was, even deeper in his debt! It was for certain her father had no intention of repaying him. And Jarad had known...

Twenty minutes later and she was parked in an out-of-the-way area—and was starting to get very angry. It was anger born of frustration and utter helplessness aided by being very much aware that she stood about as much chance of paying Jarad back his money as the moon developing purple stripes.

She had by then been through a whole gamut of emotions. How *could* her father...? How *could* Robert... And Carol—well! And what about Jarad? As angry with her family as she was, the more Merren dwelt on Jarad's role in all this, so her anger turned into fury—against him!

When she thought about it, when she'd finished reeling

from the shock of what her father had so uncaringly done—how *could* he bor...take four hundred pounds from a man he barely knew, with no intention of paying him back...? Her breath caught—she had known even less of Jarad when she had taken *two thousand* from him. She pushed that honest if unwanted reminder away—she would pay Jarad back. She would, she would. Every penny.

But what about him! He had *known* she'd be at Birchwood! He hadn't breathed a word about calling at her home on Saturday. Had even told her father not to mention his visit. And that didn't make him as pure as the driven snow, did it?

Jarad had known in advance that she would be at his New Forest house. He had known that *before* he had left London! Merren remembered his lovemaking of only that morning. Oh, how she'd thrilled to his kisses, to his touch—and he'd known where she'd be—before leaving London!

Had he planned a big seduction scene? Suddenly she felt quite ill. She couldn't bear it. Everything had been so spontaneous on her part—but Jarad? The more she thought about it, the more convinced she became that planned it he had. She remembered his, 'You'd prefer I went to a hotel?' when he'd found her there. Of course he'd never had any intention of going to a hotel! 'Do I have your permission to bring my gear in?' he'd asked—and she had actually *smiled*.

Green—they didn't come any greener than her. He *had* planned it. All along. As soon as her father had told him where she would be, Jarad had planned—the seduction. And she—she'd fallen for it! Well, almost. But he'd planned it; she could see that now. Oh, nothing rushed or hurried, nothing grabbed—he was too sophisticated for that. He was fully aware of her inexperience in matters sexual, and had obviously decided on a slow and gradual build-up, so that by this morning she would be putty in his hands.

And, for the most part, she had been. Would have continued to be—but for her subconscious plaguing her at very nearly the last moment because she owed him money. She had that last-second hiccup to thank that she had veered away from total commitment.

Jarad had planned it all along. How could it be otherwise? He had *known* she'd be there. The more she thought about it, the more furious Merren became. So much so that when a few more minutes went by she grew incensed, and nothing would do but for her to go and see him and give him a piece of her mind. He probably wouldn't be in, but as she started up her car she knew she was furious enough to park her car outside his home and wait until he did come home. Always assuming, of course, that the womanising swine did come home and wasn't intending to take his date of the evening down to the New Forest for a 'nightcap'.

A dry sob shook her, telling her, if she didn't know it, that she was overwrought. Merren sped along, aware that she shouldn't go to see him—not until she had calmed down. But since around five-thirty that morning her emotions had been on the jump, and she knew she wasn't going to feel 'right' within herself until she'd had a few short, sharp, pertinent words with one Jarad Montgomery. She knew full well she could have said those few short, sharp, pertinent words down the telephone. But that wouldn't do. That wouldn't do at all.

None of her fury had abated when she reached his smart address. Merren left her car and, placing her car keys in her bag, felt the key to Jarad's other address. She took hold of it, then stormed to ring the bell at his elegant front door.

She fully expected he would be out for the evening. But impatiently, though still prepared to wait in her car for his return, she rang his doorbell again.

The door opened, and tall, black-haired, grey-eyed—and generally pretty wonderful—Jarad stood there. Merren had lost sight in her anger of just how much she loved him. But her feelings for him rose up in her then as unexpectedly she recalled how the last time they had been together she had been naked in his arms. But, even as hot colour seared her face, Merren was reminding herself that—for goodness' sake—his near seduction of her was what this was all about.

Not waiting for him to speak, she informed him shortly, 'I need to talk to you!' the sentence unthought. If he said, Good evening, Merren. How are you? She'd hit him.

'They all say that,' he commented drolly, and she was glad he did—it refuelled her anger more than anything else could have.

'Don't get your hopes up, Montgomery!' she snapped. 'I...'

'It's obviously something that won't wait,' he interrupted coolly. But his look was all-assessing as he added, 'Since I don't normally row on my doorstep, perhaps you'd care to come in.'

At that moment she hated him. He was cool—she was boiling over. She brushed past him and, not waiting for him, charged along the hall to his drawing room. She heard the front door close, and turned to face him.

'May I offer you a drink?' he enquired, and smiled pleasantly as he added, 'You're looking—mmm—rather hot.'

'This isn't a social call!' she abruptly let him know, and, the key to Birchwood in her hand, she slammed it down on a nearby table. 'The key to your love-nest!' she flared.

Jarad came further into the room and stopped a yard or so away from her, his glance going to the key she had so angrily put down, and back to her stormy face. Then suddenly, while he looked at her, his expression softened.

'Ah, Merren,' he murmured, nothing but understanding in his gentle tone. 'You're in a state because of our love-making this morning. In your innocence you had a last-minute attack of panic and...'

'No—you...' Hurriedly she butted in. How *could* he so easily, so matter-of-factly, talk of what had taken place between them that morning? Her face was scarlet; she knew it was. 'It's g-got nothing to do with that!' she erupted, and knew she had spoken too hastily in her angry agitation—it had everything to do with that.

'You haven't come to apologise?' he enquired, his gentle tone gone to be teasing.

Apologise! She'd *kill* him! 'It's *you* who should apologise to me!' she exploded. 'You...'

'What did I do?' he interrupted, and before she could let him know, he went on, 'You're surely not objecting to the fact that now you know for certain you're a full-blooded female who...'

She stopped him right there, her voice rising. 'I already *knew* that!' she cried, outraged.

'So...?'

'What I didn't know—' she refused to let him get more than one word in '—was that it was all planned! That...'

'Planned?' he echoed, his look of understanding not staying around long, she noted.

But still she wasn't prepared to listen to a word from

him. 'That I'd been set up!' she hissed, and didn't like at all the way his eyes narrowed and he looked at her sharply. 'That...'

'Just what the devil are you talking about?' he demanded.

Almost she could have believed him. Almost she could have believed he didn't have a clue what she was talking about. But he *had* called at her home, and he *had* asked her father not to mention his visit, and her anger sought and found the spur she needed—hadn't she admitted to being greener than grass before?—oh, no, it wasn't going to happen again.

'You heard!' she answered aggressively. 'And you know!' her anger truly got out of her control when she realised that this man in front of her, who she knew was quicker on the uptake than greased lightning, now appeared to be totally foxed as to what she was talking about, and she charged into battle to hotly challenge, 'How dare you lend my father money?'

Well, he'd comprehended that quickly enough, she noticed. Though didn't thank him, nor his answer, when at first he murmured, 'So that's what this is all about.' Quite plainly he was a man averse to answering questions, more at home with asking them, and perhaps he'd been caught on the raw having his actions questioned—tough! 'As I recall it, I lent some to you, too,' he clipped.

The pig! The utter pig! She didn't need to have that thrown back at her—she guessed he'd be a perfect swine in the boardroom if the occasion demanded it. 'My father can't pay you back!' she snapped, with more anger than thought.

'Without meaning to be rude—can you?'

She'd walked into that; she knew she had. Just as she knew she was floundering out of her depth if she hoped to come off more than second best with him. But she was made of sterner stuff than to merely turn tail and—as she knew she should—get out of there.

She had come to give him a piece of her mind, and, given that he had soon gone from understanding to hostile, she wasn't moving until she had. 'Not by going to bed with you, I won't!' she hurled at him—oh, he didn't like that. She saw his face darken, but cared not. 'You didn't want my father to tell me you'd called at my home on Saturday, did you? How very kind of him to tell you where I was going. Just the spot for a little seduction w—'

'Don't be ridiculous!' he cut in angrily—and that sent her fury into orbit.

'Ridiculous!' she yelled. 'It nearly came off too, didn't it, Montgomery? We almost made love for the t-two thousand,' she stammered. She was losing it, tears near. 'What was I supposed to d-do for the extra four hundred? Or...' She broke off as he took that step nearer that brought him straight in front of her. He caught hold of her arm, his anger turning to fury; she jerked out of his grip. 'Or was that four hundred supposed to clinch it?'

'You're...'

'Ridiculous? Not from where I'm standing!' she hissed, and hated him with a vengeance when he again caught a hold of her arm. She tried to jerk free, but this time he wouldn't let her and held on to her. 'You knew I'd be there—there at Birchwood. You knew, and thought, Now there's an opportunity to get my virgin score up...'

'You're the end!' he sliced in sharply. 'You haven't any idea what you're talking about. You've deliberately and totally misconstrued my motives, and...'

'And the band played, believe *that* if you like!' she

flew, and, out of control again, she tried to jerk her left arm out of his grip, and when he stubbornly, as furious as she, refused to let her go, she did the only frustrated thing possible—she hit him across the face with her right hand.

It was a mistake, and she knew it the moment her hand cracked against his skin. Even if she didn't regret it, she knew she shouldn't have done it. Jarad wasn't the sort of man to take that kind of treatment without wanting retribution. Grey eyes blazed into her sparking blue eyes, his chin jutted—and the next she knew he had caught hold of her other arm and was bringing her inexorably closer.

'No!' she gasped, as his head came nearer and his intent dawned on her.

But he was taking no heed. 'Since I can't return the compliment, you'll have to take this instead!' he snarled—and, giving her no time for verbal retaliation, he took possession of her mouth with his own in an angry kiss.

She didn't want him to kiss her like that. She kicked out at him, but missed. 'D…' was as far as she managed to get by way of protest when he broke his kiss, then, as she pushed at him, enraged, he kissed her again.

She fought him, punched where she could—which wasn't easy since he still had hold of both her arms—and she still didn't want him to kiss her like that. His kisses of that morning had started out gently before passion had flared between them. Now his kisses were angry, hostile—and held no liking, let alone the love she craved for.

Love! Was she stupid or what? She pushed violently. 'Cut it out, Montgomery!' she erupted when she had the chance—only while there was now a degree of daylight between their bodies, he still had a hold of her arms.

'When I'm ready!' he answered, a mocking note penetrating his anger with her. 'You started this, Shepherd, at least have the decency to let me finish it.'

'Decency!' She refused to bow down, to beg to be released. 'What do you know about d...?' He read the end, and put his own full-stop to her sentence by once more claming her lips with his own.

Only this time his anger seemed to be draining away from him. While the touch of his mouth on hers had started out aggressively enough, a gentle, more persuasive suggestion was beginning to take over.

And the, 'St-stop at once!' which she ordered when she could, didn't, to her ears, sound as forceful as it should.

Grey eyes, no longer blazing, stared down at her. 'Ask me nicely?' he requested.

'Go to blazes!' she found a modicum of spirit to fire at him—and didn't have chance to say anything for quite some while after that, because Jarad was claiming her lips again, only this time his aggressiveness had disappeared and his kiss was gentle—giving, not taking—and Merren was starting to grow confused.

Somehow his hands had left her arms and his arms were around her. He parted her lips with his own, and when she could have pushed him away—could then, she knew, have got free—Merren found instead that she was melting against him. All at once she was responding, finding heaven once more in his arms.

'Jarad.' She even whispered his name, her aggressiveness, like his, departed.

He kissed her and she kissed him, rejoicing once more in his touch, in his hold. This haven was where she wanted to be, a fire starting in her again as his strong, manly arms held her as his long, sensitive fingers caressed her spine.

He held her close to him; she pressed even closer. She heard a groan of desire leave him, and that was all right by her, because she'd had a confusing day, and an even more confusing and miserable hour or so of it, and to be with him like this was the solace she needed.

'Little love,' he murmured against the skin of her throat, and she gloried in the endearment.

His hands caressed her ribcage, tenderly moving to capture first one breast and then the other. She clutched on to him as his gentle fingers found the hardened peaks of her breasts, sending tremors of delight through her.

He took her with him to one of the sofas in the room, all hostility forgotten as he undid the fastenings of her dress and without haste let it slip to the floor. 'Shy?' he teased when she went in close for a second or two, so he should not see her. She stretched up and kissed him, mindless, then, to the fact that only that morning he had seen far more of her.

Merren didn't know how she came to be lying with Jarad on that sofa in such close harmony; she could only thrill to the wonder of it, her emotions asunder. She needed Jarad so—not just physically, she needed his strong arms about her. Since falling in love with him it had become a bleak world out there without him.

Kiss after wonderful kiss they shared. They exchanged more kisses, passion soaring. Her bra seemed to have disappeared—likewise his shirt. She stared, fascinated, at his broad manly chest, and he was equally fascinated by her silken pink-tipped breasts. Tenderly he traced the full roundness of her left breast, teasing the hardened tip until Merren quivered with her desire for him. Jarad bent and took that pink peak between his lips, and with a choky breath of wanting she pressed against him.

Such was her love for him, such was the nonsense he had made of her thinking power. Merren had forgotten everything but their two selves when Jarad moved over her, pressing her into the softness of the sofa. Soon, she knew, either there or perhaps in one of the upstairs rooms, they would become as one.

Jarad kissed her once more, his wonderful hands coming to her behind, pulling her to him as she pressed against him. A sound of wanting left him, and, because she loved him so, Merren felt she had to tell him how it was with her.

She wanted to tell him of the depth of her love for him, but somehow felt shy too, though shyness, she owned, was unbelievable in the circumstances. She opened her mouth. 'I...'

Jarad pulled back to look at her, his expression tender. 'You...?' he coaxed softly.

'I—want you,' she sighed.

He gently kissed her. But again pulled back to look at her. 'You're sure, Merren?' he asked urgently.

She wondered how he could ask such a thing. Wasn't it obvious? She hesitated, confused suddenly in this new world she had only shaken hands with that morning, but in which she was again up to her ears. 'I—er...' was about as much as she could manage.

But she didn't need to say anything more, apparently. Jarad had seen her hesitation, and, putting his own construction on it, was—to her absolute horror—rapidly moving away from her! Even as she watched he turned his back on her, and was already shrugging into his shirt.

She opened her mouth to call his name, to repeat that she wanted him, wildly she wanted him, and that there was no hesitation about that. Yes, she'd been a bit confused, but...

But she didn't get the chance. 'You'd better go,' Jarad decided tersely.

'Go?' she echoed. She wanted him still, wanted his arms back around her. He couldn't, just couldn't be meaning it! But, apparently, he was.

'Go now,' he instructed her grittily.

For several stunned seconds Merren just stared at his back. And then, through her bewilderment, pride began to stir. And, having stirred, was suddenly blasting off to rocket upwards. He was telling her to go! Never would she have believed she would have waited around in such circumstances to be told *twice* to leave. He was throwing her out! *Her!* Actually throwing *her* out!

Merren was getting her clothes on even as she started to move. She wasn't staying around to be told a third time! Sorely then did she need a 'get-out' line. But her stunned brain just didn't seem capable of helping her.

Her dress was on, her shoes were on—though she couldn't remember even having parted from her shoes—and, in haste, she was on her way. Without saying another word, Merren got out of there.

She was grateful for those few minutes when she seemed to have a non-functioning brain. Because as she automatically drove in the direction of her home, when her brain did begin to work, and the power of thought returned, it was all too excruciatingly painful.

Now she knew what being rejected felt like. It was no good saying she should never have put herself in that position—once Jarad's kisses had ceased to be angry, she had been lost.

Merren drove on, her mind in torment. He, Jarad, the man she loved, had rejected her! She had been his for the taking—and he had said no thank you. As she, that morning had told him no, and had rejected him, so he had returned the courtesy and had rejected her.

Her thoughts at that point started to become mixed up again, and she pulled over and stopped her car while she sorted herself out. Because suddenly she was realising that, whereas this morning some subconscious prodding about the money she owed Jarad had prevented her from becoming his, tonight—just now—her subconscious had played dead. How that was possible when everything that had gone on this evening had grown initially from the fact she owed Jarad that money, she just didn't know.

She knew very little, she reflected some long while later. Though Jarad had accused her of deliberately and totally misconstruing his motives, she couldn't see what other motive he'd had for telling her father not to mention his visit to her home on Saturday. Jarad *had* had seduction in mind when he'd joined her at Birchwood. She was sure about that. What she wasn't so sure about was whether, because of her rejection of him, Jarad, while making love to her tonight had decided to let her know what it felt like to be the one spurned.

With thoughts of money, seduction and rejection spinning around in her head, Merren had started up her car and was on her way again when she knew that she didn't want to go home. Her father, her brother and her sister-in-law were at home, and she wasn't ready to see them again. Apart from anything else, the house she had grown up in didn't feel like home any more.

Had she the money, she felt she might have booked herself into a hotel. That foul word 'money' had reared its ugly head again! She was more determined than ever to pay Jarad back what she—and her father—owed him. He could whistle if he wanted her to be his pretend girlfriend again. A shaky breath took her as she faced the unlikelihood of that happening.

She was never gong to see Jarad again, but pay him back she would. She would scrimp and save, get a weekend job, and hoard every penny, the sooner to have that debt paid. Which rendered spending money on overnight hotel accommodation—in the hope she would feel more like seeing her family in the morning—out of the question. It was instinctive after that for her to drive to the cottage of the man who had always been more of a father to her than her own father.

'I thought that was your car I heard.' Her uncle Amos beamed at her when he opened the door to her.

'I wasn't sure if you'd still be up,' she commented.

'I've a problem I'm trying to solve,' he replied, his glance taking in her pallor and the general look of her. 'Come in, sweetheart, come in, and let me see if I can solve yours.'

Was it so obvious? Merren followed her uncle into his sitting room, noting absently that the drop-leave table was fully open and was covered with a large and complicated-looking drawing, while various other papers bearing mathematical equations far above her head were scattered there too.

'I'm sorry to disturb you,' she apologised. 'I just— wondered if there's any chance I could stay here tonight. I can sleep on the sofa,' she added hastily.

And had never loved her uncle more when, to her astonishment, he quietly revealed, 'My dear, I cleared out all of the junk from the spare bedroom the moment I knew you'd been invaded by Robert and his family. The room's been ready for you since then.'

'Oh, Uncle,' she whispered, and had to fight hard to hold back tears.

'If it's the bad, I'd better make you a pot of tea,' he teased her, and she found a smile for him.

They were drinking tea when Merren stirred herself to realise that, though she didn't want to return home there were still certain manners to be observed. 'I should ring home and tell them where I am,' she stated despondently.

'Would you like me to do it?'

It was the truth she didn't feel like speaking to either her father or Robert herself, but she didn't think it fair to let her uncle do it for her. 'I couldn't let...' Her lovely uncle already had the phone in his hand and was dialling.

Merren gathered from her uncle's tone that it was her father who answered the phone, for, barely hiding his dislike of his brother-in-law, Amos Yardley informed him, 'Merren's staying the night with me. And if I have my way, she'll stay with me until she has her house back.' And that was it; he put the phone down, and actually grinned at her when he saw she looked slightly startled. 'You thought I was a bit blunt?' he queried wickedly.

'Well, I...'

'You'd have been kinder? Of course you would. But I've known your father longer than you. He invented "give me an inch and I'll take a yard".' But his grin disappeared. 'Your brother's just like him. While you take after your mother, Robert's your father all over again.'

'Robert's having a tough time of it just now,' Merren attempted to defend.

'And so are you, love,' Amos Yardley answered quietly. 'Care to tell me what's troubling you so?'

'I—can't.' Love her uncle as she did, her love for Jarad, his rejection of her, was intensely private.

But her uncle was not to be put off. 'I'm not prying

purely for the sake of it, my dear, believe me. But I'm too fond of you to let you go to bed so upset when I may be able to help.'

'Oh, Uncle,' Merren found a tired smile. 'You're already helping by letting me stay here.'

He ignored that, and, his logical inventor's mind delving, he went to the very core of the problem. 'It's got something to do with money, hasn't it?' And, when she could not deny it, 'You were doing all right before your brother and his brood and then your father moved in.' Although Merren had always known that he was a clever man, her uncle showed himself far more discerning than she had realised when he stated, 'They're both hard up, probably draining the housekeeping.' And, his look sharp, he added, 'They want you to sell your mother's ring, don't they? They think they're perfectly entitled to a share.'

Merren stared sadly at him. He knew how much that ring had meant to her. 'Oh, Uncle Amos—I've already sold it,' she cried.

Caught at her most vulnerable, at his gentle coaxing Merren found her defences crumbling, her strength to pretend that all was right with her world gone. Bit by tiny bit, her uncle got from her how she'd sold the ring, how she'd been mugged and robbed of the money outside Jarad's home.

'I liked him,' Amos Yardley opined. But Merren loved Jarad, still she loved him, reject her though he had; her love for him would not go away—she wished it would; the pain was almost physical. 'Did he help you?' her uncle asked, and Merren found she was confessing Jarad's financial help in all of this. 'That was a couple of months ago?' her uncle documented.

'About that,' she agreed.

'So what happened tonight that's distressed you so?'

She couldn't tell him. She couldn't tell anyone of her love for Jarad, but found she was telling her uncle of her discovery that her father had increased her debt to him. 'I've just been to see Jarad,' she ended.

And realised her discerning uncle must have seen how she felt about Jarad, for he sympathised, 'Poor love, you care for him, and you've quarrelled over the money he gave your father,' seeming, like her, to know her father would regard the money as a gift, and not a loan.

'Something like that,' she mumbled.

'Well, we can't mend it tonight, so I suggest bed, a good night's sleep, and we'll see what repairs we can make in the morning.'

Merren did not sleep well. She went over and over the frustration of her father getting her further and further into debt with Jarad. She went round in circles with that frustration—and also how, because Jarad had kept quiet about knowing she would be at Birchwood—and had asked her father to keep quiet about it—she had become furious with him. She was torn apart again and again as she recalled Jarad's rejection of her. And her uncle thought they might make repairs in the morning! As clever as he was, Merren couldn't see how.

She was up early; so was Amos Yardley. To her surprise he was not dressed in his usual working overalls, but had on a crisp white shirt, and had donned his one and only suit. 'I've no need to ask how you didn't sleep,' he teased gently, his glance taking in the shadows beneath her eyes. 'I've had a problematical night myself,' he confessed.

'Your latest invention isn't working out?'

'That wasn't my problem. But it's now sorted in my

head. So, young lady, are you going to do your uncle a favour and have the day off work?'

Merren blinked. 'Why would I need a day off work?' She started to smile. 'I'm perfectly h...'

'Because I need to go out and attend to some business, and it would please me very much if you'd go and pack your belongings from the address where you used to live and move your things in here.' Merren stared at him. It was true, she felt no more like going home this morning than she had last night, but... 'And I'd just love it if we could have one of those roasts for dinner like your mother used to make. You won't have time to do all of that if you go to work.'

Merren looked at him, this dear man who'd been like a father to her. She thought of her workload at the office. They weren't too busy just now, and somebody else could easily cover her for one day. Did she want to move in with Uncle Amos? It suddenly seemed the best idea she'd heard in a long while!

'You're on,' she smiled.

'For everything?'

Day off work, collecting her clothes, moving in, cooking a roast? 'Everything,' she agreed.

'That's my girl.'

Merren had a busy morning. She was glad to be busy. She needed to be busy. Thoughts of Jarad, who just wouldn't stay out of her head, were driving her to distraction. She first took advantage of her uncle being out and attending to the business he had spoken of to give his house a thorough cleaning, taking care not to move any of his paperwork—while it might look like a jumble to her, he obviously knew where everything was.

At five minutes past nine she took time out to ring her

office, and, explaining she was well but needed the day off, arranged with her boss to have a holiday day.

Once the house had been de-cobwebbed, scrubbed and polished—she'd tackled the windows that afternoon—Merren drove to her home of yesterday. Neither her father nor her brother seemed in any way put out that she was moving. Though Carol was sweet and said she would miss her. 'Not that I blame you for going—I can't think how you've put up with us so long,' Carol went on. 'But I can't help feeling guilty that we've driven you out of your home.'

'It was never mine, only borrowed,' Merren answered, thinking how the house had always belonged to her father, and—given that she had always lived there—how he, and his son and family had every bit as much of a right to live there as her.

In that thought, however, she found she was entirely mistaken. Her uncle had returned by the time, via a supermarket, she got back. Seeing his car, she left her cases in her own car and went in to see him.

He had changed from his suit to his usual outfit. 'Sit down, Merren,' he said as soon as he saw her, 'I have something to tell you.' Her cases stayed in her car for quite some while, as he began his first startling revelation, explaining that the house she and her mother had lived in belonged to him, and not her father.

'You own it!' Merren stared at him in utter amazement. 'Not my father?'

'Oh, he thought he did. He hot-footed it up here to check as soon as he could when he received a letter from you saying something about all of you living in his house. He thought I'd signed it over to your mother, and calculated that, if she hadn't made a will before she died so unexpectedly, since they'd never divorced, the house would automatically go to him. I gave him short shrift on that one.'

'You own it,' Merren repeated, trying to adjust her long-held notion that her mother's brother was next door to penury.

'I always intended your mother should have it,' he answered. 'I bought it for her when I could see Lewis Shepherd was never going to provide for her. When he started to treat her so shabbily—forgive me, my dear, it's because he's your father that I've held my tongue over a lot of things, but he was not the best husband in the world to my sister—I wanted to make certain that he couldn't sell the house over her head.'

'But you own it,' Merren repeated again, as she started to recover from being stunned.

'It was my intention, when your mother died, to have the house signed over to you. But even though you hadn't seen your father for some while I was certain he'd wriggle out of the woodwork at some time and begin leeching on you. I've been remiss, most remiss,' he went on. 'Instead of just asking if you were all right for money, I should have done something about it.' He smiled a loving smile. 'I've spent this morning taking care of that.' Merren discovered that her shocks for the day were not yet over when he continued, 'I've been to my solicitors and drawn up a will in your favour, and I've been to your bank and deposited ten thousand pounds in your account.' Merren just stared speechlessly at him, and he added, 'I'll give the same amount to your brother—your mother would want me to do that.'

'But—but I didn't know you had any money!' Merren gasped—and her uncle chuckled.

'Because I more often than not look like a tramp? I have one suit,' he informed her. 'Why would I need another? I'm comfortable with myself as I am. I go to see manufacturers about twice a year, and if they're that interested in my inventions they can come to see me.'

'Your...you have people interested...?'

'Frequently,' her uncle smiled. 'In fact, I do quite nicely,' he said modestly, and Merren felt extremely guilty that she had never known, for he had never said nor boasted—though that wouldn't be his way—that he had sold any of his inventions. 'So you see, my dear, I do have a little money.'

'Yes, but...' she was still having trouble taking it in. 'I can't take your money, Uncle. You m...'

'Did you not hear me, Merren?' he asked, severely for him. 'You are my heir. I see no good reason not to let you have a little in advance now that you need it. In fact, but for the certainty your father will take and take from you, I'd make it more.'

'Can you afford ten—no, twenty thousand pounds?' she asked, still finding all he had revealed totally incredible.

'Oh, yes,' he answered. 'Believe me, I can.'

With that Merren had to be satisfied, though she did have another question. 'Why did my mother never mention that you owned the house we lived in?' she asked.

'Because your mother was the lovable person she was, she would have done everything to prevent you knowing what a rotten husband, father and provider Lewis Shepherd was,' her uncle answered. 'It just wasn't in her to blacken his name to you.'

Merren looked at him, and suddenly comprehended something else. 'It wasn't my father who sent her money those times when things got a bit tight, was it?'

'Your mother was an extremely proud woman, Merren—as you are,' he answered. 'She would only allow me to do so much. Now,' he said, brightening suddenly, 'haven't you got a cheque you want to make out before you get started on my dinner?'

'Oh, Uncle!' Merren exclaimed softly, as his meaning hit her. She left her seat and went to kiss his cheek. 'Thank you,' she said from her heart.

She was far from adjusting to everything he had told her when he left her to go to his workshop. Or to the fact she now had ten thousand pounds in her bank account. But at that moment Jarad returned to dominate her head, and she realised that now she had the wherewithal to repay him.

Her head was buzzing when she went to her car to bring in her belongings. Because the cottage was small, Merren hadn't packed all of her possessions. But up in her new room she found her writing paper and cheque-book, and was in a torn—every-way kind of dilemma over the best way to go about repaying Jarad.

She knew she was being pathetic, but even after the way they had parted, the way he just rejected her, she felt a quite desperate need to see him again. And had to wonder then—was that part of the reason she had gone to see him last night? She had been angry, she recalled, furious even—but in there somewhere had her old enemy subconscious been having another little go?

At that moment her pride reared up to give her a little nip. For goodness' sake, was she actually contemplating going to see him again—after the way he'd rejected her last night? Pull yourself together, girl, do.

Merren pulled herself together, but couldn't help lingering on his name as she wrote 'Jarad Montgomery' on the cheque. The cheque was easily written, but her letter was started many times. In the end, she settled for:

Dear Jarad,
I believe the enclosed ends matters between us.
With grateful thanks.
Yours sincerely, Merren.

She addressed an envelope to him and placed her note
and her cheque for two thousand four hundred pounds
inside. Then went swiftly to the post, her fingers holding
on to the envelope for several hesitating seconds before,
impatient with herself, she let the envelope drop into the
box. It was done, finished—and she wished she felt better, but she didn't.

Merren went to her office the next morning, still adjusting to the knowledge that her impoverished uncle was
in fact quite well to do, and, having severed all connection with Jarad, tried to pick up the threads of her life.

Not that ending all need for contact would matter a
light to him! He'd probably put her cheque to one side
and bank it some time when he thought of it—and forget
all about her. It hurt, and she ached for him, and wondered when, if ever, that pain would go away.

She drove to her new home after work with Jarad in
her every thought. She cooked dinner with Jarad domi-
nating her mind, and had him still there while she conversed with her uncle over the meal.

Jarad remained in her head when, after dinner, her uncle went back to his workshop. Had Jarad received her
letter yet? He should have done. Though if he worked
late, or perhaps was away on business, he wouldn't
have... The ringing of the telephone cut through her
thoughts.

She looked at the instrument, thought about calling her
uncle. But it could be a wrong number, so why disturb
him? She went over to the instrument and picked it up.

'Hello?' she enquired. And had her ears blasted for her trouble.

'Where did you get the money?' Jarad bellowed.

Shattered, Merren pulled the receiver away from her ear. She had yearned to hear the sound of his voice—for *this*? 'Not by selling my body!' she yelled back at him—and a moment later she slammed down the phone.

Who did he think he was? Merren found she was shaking. Oh, Lord, was there no end to it? Why did he have to phone? And phone here! He must have contacted her old home and been told that she was now living with her uncle. Not that it mattered.

Nothing seemed to matter very much any more. Well, not to her. He, one Jarad Montgomery, obviously felt his nose pushed out of joint because he had lost the cover of his 'steady girlfriend'. Well, tough. She didn't care, not any more.

Which, she realised, some time later, the washing-up done, the house spick and span again, was just so much nonsense. She did care, and it was too late now to wish she'd answered differently, had perhaps had some kind of amicable discussion with him. But there had been no hope of that. Jarad had affected her temper from the first. If only she could have that telephone call over again. But he wouldn't phone again; she knew that for a fact.

Nor did he phone. But just then, while her uncle was still fully absorbed in his workshop at the rear, the front doorbell imperiously sounded, and when Merren went to answer it she found she did have the chance to be nicer to the man she loved. Because when she opened the door, who should she see standing there—but Jarad Montgomery?

She felt her face flush with colour, her emotions instantly in an uproar. But one look at his unsmiling, aggressive countenance, and any chance of being all sweetness and light went rapidly from her. She might be head over heels in love with the brute, but he looked ready to go for her jugular—so she got in first.

'Come to insult me in person?' she fired aggressively.

'Where did you get it?' he demanded.

'That's none of your business!'

'I'm making it my business!' he snarled.

'Pfff!' she scorned, just as though she didn't absolutely adore him. 'How?' it was her turn to demand. How did he think he could make it his business?

Jarad hesitated—very unlike him, she realised, but she still wasn't prepared to give an inch. Had that magnificent mouth really kissed hers? 'I've grown to l...like you,' he answered at last—and her legs went like water.

But she was her mother's proud daughter, and, weak-as-water legs or not, Merren had no intention of being rejected a second time—not that Jarad looked as if he desired her, more that he desired that she finish out their 'contract'.

'Well, that makes everything lovely, doesn't it?' she jibed—and was left standing when he stepped over her uncle's threshold and inside the cottage. Come in—why don't you? 'I don't recall inviting...' she began, but was left gasping when Jarad closed the front door and turned back to her, his eyes looking not a tiny bit more friendly.

'We're past inviting, you and me,' he told her toughly, and while her heart started hammering at the purposeful, determined look to him, 'We'll talk,' he decreed—and strode from her into the sitting room—leaving Merren gaping after him.

CHAPTER EIGHT

MERREN knew there was little she could do but follow Jarad into her uncle's sitting room. But, while her heart was pounding against her ribs at seeing Jarad, at having him so near, she realised, for her own sake, that whatever it was he thought they had to talk about she was going to oppose him all the way.

He was tall, and seemed to fill the sitting room as he turned and stood facing her when she joined him. She wanted to swallow on a knot of emotion, but wouldn't. 'I won't ask you to take a seat—this obviously isn't going to take long,' she opened for belligerent starters.

Whatever he was thinking Jarad managed to keep in check, but his glance was not the most friendly she had ever seen. 'I trust you've not been consorting with loan sharks?' he questioned curtly.

'I had never thought to do so—though I'd sooner pay their interest charges than yours,' she responded waspishly.

'When did I ask for interest?' he rapped, and she could have hit him.

'You know full well what I mean!' she flew.

'And you know full well that sex never came into the agreement,' he rapped.

Merren felt warm colour come up under her skin—trust him to bring out into the open the very thing which she would prefer not to mention! 'Well, you've been paid back now so—er—we're quits!' she snapped. 'I've

165

thanked you very much…' her tone altered a trifle '…and I was, and am, very grateful, as I said in my note, but…'

'You also said in your note that your cheque, "ends matters between us",' he quoted. And looking her straight in the eye, he said firmly, 'Well, I'm here, Merren Shepherd, to tell you it doesn't.'

She blinked. 'You want interest? I'll give you interest.'

His eyes narrowed. 'I've taken enough of your insults!' he gritted.

'Tough!'

He ignored her. 'Matters are far from ended between you and me, Merren. You know…'

'You're miffed!' she butted in. 'I spoilt your plans for a quiet life and you don't like it.' She was crumbling inside; he mustn't know it. 'You're miffed because I've decided not to be your pretend girlfriend any more and…'

'That's got nothing to do with it!'

'Much! You th-thought that until your brother came back you'd got cover from your mother wanting you to settle down. You…'

'Were that true it would be hilarious.'

Merren stared at him. She was flummoxed. 'Which bit?'

Jarad stared back at her and seemed to relent a little. He looked far less aggressive, anyhow, when he conceded, 'It's true Piers will be away for a year, and it's true my mother—with her able assistant Veda—diverted her attentions to me and my bachelor state the moment Piers took off.' He paused, and then, his look steady on her, added, 'But, believe me, their attentions to my lack of a wife were nothing I couldn't cope with.'

Merren's mouth fell open. 'Take a seat,' she suggested, but more because she was feeling quite shaky in the leg area than anything else. Jarad waited until she was seated in the one easy chair, and then availed himself of the small sofa. 'You're trying to make out *now*—when I've put up with you for more than one weekend,' she inserted, trying to make it sound as if that had been a hardship, 'that none of it was necessary? That I...?'

'Oh, I wouldn't say it was unnecessary,' he countered. She didn't need to be mystified, she was having enough problems just trying to stay clear-headed. 'From your point of view, I judged it was very necessary.'

'Too kind!' She attempted sarcasm—it was a poor thing.

'I knew, when you came to see me the day after I let you have two thousand pounds, that there was an honesty, a pride in you, which meant you weren't feeling good about taking the money, that you'd feel much better if I could think up some way for you to earn it.'

'Yet another favour!' Merren said sharply—oh, she loved him so—and was terrified it might show. 'You told me to come and see you the next day!'

'But expected to see neither you nor the money again,' he said, to her amazement. She supposed her surprise must be showing, for he smiled suddenly, and she felt all wobbly inside—and had to concentrate really hard because of it.

'So you dreamed up the idea of the "pretend girl-friend" job?'

'I should not have,' he admitted. 'But there you were, wanting a job, and there was my mother with that look in her eyes when she saw you—having just heard me state the good news that I was seeing someone special—and it didn't take a second to see how I could work everything to my advantage.'

'While at the same time you were giving me a way to

repay you—a kind of job,' Merren quickly worked out. 'And into the bargain it cut out the risk of you offending your mother when you refused to co-operate with any social plans she had in mind for you.'

'Something along those lines,' he agreed. 'But I have to confess it was more for a bit of devilment than anything else that I started down a road whose many junctions took me by surprise.'

Having worked out why he had given her the 'job' he had, Merren's brain seemed to have been used up. 'My brain's in hibernation,' she hinted—though naturally with an outward show of being barely interested.

Jarad looked at her levelly. She had a panicky idea she had been perhaps just a shade too off-hand. But, as ever, he wasn't leaving anything lurking in dark corners. After perhaps another moment or two of seriously contemplating her, he asked quietly, 'Why are you so against me, Merren?' She swallowed, her insides churning. Had she by her very indifference given herself away? His look was certainly more than speculative anyway, when he went on, 'All I did was to stop kissing you. Is that the reason you're so...?'

'Don't be ridiculous!' She sharply bounced back a phrase he'd used on her once.

He smiled a smile she wished she understood, but she was grateful when he decided not to pursue the subject, but went back to the discussion they'd been having. 'Contrary to anything I may have said or indicated,' he resumed, 'I promise you, Merren, all lies and half-truths between you and me are a thing of the past—I am, and always have been, more than able to cope with my mother's attempts to get me to "settle down".'

'You're referring to the various women your mother introduced...?'

'Exactly,' he agreed, then paused. 'I had absolutely no problem with any of that,' he went on, and, his eyes holding, refusing to let her look away, 'My problems began, Merren,' he added, 'on the day I met you.'

She had no earthly idea what he could be meaning, but with her heart misbehaving and her insides churning, her brain didn't seem to be doing much to help her comprehend either. 'It stands to reason that if anybody's at fault here, it has to be me,' she managed—and got the shock of her life when Jarad moved to the end of the sofa to be within touching distance. Then reached and took a hold of her hand.

While more of her senses joined in the general free-for-all inside her, he said, 'You keep your family together the way you have—and talk of fault!' Merren stared at him, and didn't know quite where she was when taking her other hand in his, he urged, 'Come here.' And when she didn't comply he brought her to her feet, and, leaning forward, he gently kissed her. Her legs went like water again, so that she was glad to sit down—only now she found that she was sitting on the small two-seated sofa with Jarad—and there was a veritable riot going on inside her!

'Would you like some coffee?' she asked, purely because she felt the need to say something, and that seemed about the most sensible thing she could come up with.

Jarad smiled softly, and shook his head. 'I want us to talk, my dear,' he stated—that 'my dear' making her all wobbly again.

'Oh, yes,' she mumbled, this time doing away with phony indifference—he was too sharp by half. 'You were saying…' She broke off, striving to remember what he had been saying before that lovely gentle kiss had sent her witless. 'About—about your problems beginning…'

'On the day I met you,' Jarad finished for her. 'I'll forever regret my initial cynicism on that day, my disbelief that you'd been mugged.'

'You were a pig—to begin with,' she recalled, starting to get herself more of one piece.

'I wouldn't deny it,' he totally disarmed her. 'In my defence, though, it was less than a month since Piers had brought home another victim who—once she'd had her financial loss made good—turned out to be as fit as a flea when she tried to make off with a few portable antiques into the bargain.'

Merren stared at him, slightly shaken. 'No *wonder* you were wary!'

'Not for long,' he answered. 'Your proud dignity when you said you wouldn't touch a penny of my money got through to me. And only two days later, when I don't know any female *that* special—though I pretend to my mother I do—I gradually started to realise—oh, yes, I do.'

Her throat went dry. Was Jarad saying he thought her special? He couldn't be. Could he? She couldn't ask. Couldn't bear the humiliation if he had a coronary through laughing so much. Then she remembered the glamorous Isadora Thomas—and Merren knew it was she who was being ridiculous.

'Yes, well,' she said, wishing she could put some distance between them on the short sofa, but stuck where she was. Unless she wanted this sharp man beside her to guess at her inner agitation, she was forced to stay where she was. 'Well—er—I've repaid you now,' she hinted. Perhaps he'd go—yet, even green-eyed with jealousy at the thought of him and Isadora Thomas, she wanted him to stay.

Her cool tone was not lost on him, she saw. And there

was not the smallest smile about him, when, looking firmly at her, he stated, 'That money was never an issue, Merren.'

'It wasn't?' She wanted him back smiling, gentle, kind.

'I didn't give a thought to it,' he answered. 'It didn't matter.' He took a long breath, every bit as if needing to steady himself, though why he should be in need of steadying himself, she couldn't think. Nor was she thinking, but staring, when quietly he informed her, 'What mattered to me was that *you* were starting to matter to me.'

Her eyes went huge in her face. 'I—was?' Was that squeaky voice hers?

'I kept thinking about you,' he owned carefully, causing her heartbeat to go into overdrive. 'The more I saw of you, the more I found I wanted to see you.'

'You did?' She swallowed hard, couldn't help it.

'I did,' he answered, his tone taut. 'Even when I was fooling myself we had this arrangement, so I'd have to see you, I came over and asked you to have dinner with me—purely because I wanted to take you out.'

'You didn't?' She couldn't believe it.

'I did,' he argued. 'And you had the nerve to tell me you'd already got a date. But, what did I expect? You're rather a wonderful person, Merren.'

Oh, Jarad, don't—you'll have me on my knees! She wanted to find some kind of a joke, some kind of a I'll-bet-you-say-that-to-all-of-the-girls type of comment. But it just wouldn't come. Instead, she grabbed at all of her courage and, her heart drumming away, asked, 'Wh—what, exactly, are you saying, Jarad?'

He looked at her, and there was that gentle air about him when first, he leaned forward and tenderly placed a kiss to the corner of her mouth, and then he told her quietly, 'I'm saying, Merren, that the more I've learned about you, the more I've grown to know what a lovely person you are. I'm saying that you have greater power to make me laugh and feel more light-hearted than anyone I know. I've taken you to meet my family and—when previously I'd have said I'd run a mile from any such entanglement—I've found I've enjoyed being paired with you, in the relationship we're supposed to have.' His expression had become grave when he went on, 'You once queried, did I want to go on with this pretence of us being serious about each other—it was then I began to realise that I wasn't pretending, that I was starting to become *very* serious about you.'

Her breath caught. Oh, heavens! She still wasn't sure what he was saying. What she *was* sure about was that she was close to giving herself away. And she mustn't; she mustn't! Her mouth felt dry. She remembered how much he enjoyed being footloose and fancy-free—and somehow, although her voice was husky, she managed to question, 'You—um—fought it, of course?'

'Of course,' he answered without the smallest equivocation. 'I parted from you once with a trite "Love you", and went on my way thinking, You'll have to watch that, Montgomery, you've never said that to any woman before. And since Monday when, with my head in turmoil, I left you at Birchwood, I've fought against what has become a very serious situation.'

'Oh,' Merren murmured chokily—Jarad had known some of the same turmoil that had swamped her on Monday! And—help her, someone—what was he meaning by bringing that word 'love' into it?

'You sound as shaken as I was feeling,' Jarad observed softly. She wouldn't answer, felt terrified to—just one word and he might know! But she was watching him, wide-eyed, when, after a moment, he went on, 'I left you on Monday morning with my brain an emotional quagmire—I wanted you. You wanted me. Had I frightened you? The emotions you aroused in me made me feel vulnerable, and I didn't want to feel vulnerable—and while I spent the whole of that day with you in my head, the next I knew, you were storming into my home accusing me of deliberately setting out to seduce you. That night, after you'd gone, I knew.'

'You—knew?' she asked hesitantly—he would have to tell her; she was feeling too brain-numbed to attempt to work out what it was that he knew.

Jarad looked at her solemnly, and then, raising a tender hand to trail the back of it down the side of her face, he answered, 'I knew, that night, that which I had been trying to hide from knowing for quite some while,' and causing her to stare at him, her eyes saucer-wide, her heart thundering energetically, he sincerely added, 'I knew, my dear, sweet Merren—that I was in love with you.'

'Oh!' she exclaimed, her voice jerky, staccato.

'I was shaken too.' Jarad smiled. 'I've been in a ferment about you since then. The last time we were together you left my home hating me, and I knew I should give you space to cool down. But I came home tonight knowing that if I wasn't to endure another sleepless night I was going to have to see you, to discuss us.' *Us!* She felt all trembly inside, and was still scared to say a word lest she awoke from this wonderful dream she was having. 'But what do I find when I get in but a letter from you telling me it's all ended?' He gently kissed her, and seemed to draw encouragement when she did not object, for he smiled deep into her eyes and told her bluntly, 'I wasn't having that!'

Merren smiled back, never wanting to awake. 'You must have phoned my old home.'

'I dialled without pausing to think.'

'My father told you I was now living with Uncle Amos?'

'He said there was more room here. Do you love me?'

The question was unexpected, though a moment later and Merren was realising that she could have expected it. 'As—like there's no tomorrow,' she answered shyly.

Jarad's arms came about her, and he drew her up close against his heart. 'I love you, beautiful Merren,' he murmured. 'Can you not say it?'

'I—love you,' she whispered tremulously—and felt the pressure of his arms about her increase.

'Oh, Merren,' he breathed, 'I thought there could be a chance you cared when you were so aggressive with me just now.'

'Telling you not to be ridiculous,' she took up dreamily.

His head came that little bit nearer, and he kissed her, kissed and held her, and for an age seemed content to sit with his arms around her, just holding her close to him.

Then, after minutes of holding and delighting in each other, he was pulling back a little way, looking adoringly into her warm, deeply blue eyes. 'When did you know?' he asked softly.

'That...?' Her voice failed her.

'You've gone shy on me,' he teased gently, but rephrased his question. 'When did you know about this all-consuming emotion which creeps up on one all unsuspecting, and takes over? When, sweetheart, did you know you loved me?'

She smiled softly, but owned, 'Well, there were indications along the way.'

'As in?' he insisted on knowing.

'As in—I never used to have a temper before I met you, but you were constantly disturbing my equilibrium.'

'And?' he asked cheerfully.

'And, while I wasn't admitting it at the time, I felt quite sick with jealousy when I saw that picture of you with Isadora Thomas in the paper.'

'You were jealous?' He seemed quite taken with the idea, Merren thought—he was smiling anyhow—and had to smile herself. 'You're adorable,' he said tenderly, but, to her enchantment, confessed, 'Would it make things better if I told you that asking Isadora Thomas out was purely a counter-measure because you were in my head so much?'

'Honestly?' Good heavens!

'Instinct must have been telling me I was at risk.' He smiled. 'But jealousy isn't your sole prerogative, sweet Merren.'

Again she stared at him, thrilled to her being with every confession he made of how things were with him. 'You've been jealous too?' she asked. 'Who...?'

'You need to ask?' he scolded with mock severity, but went on to surprise her further by admitting, 'Had I truly wanted to, I could have got out of taking you down to Hillmount...'

'You could?'

'You were getting to me, Miss Shepherd,' he acknowledged lovingly. 'Somehow I'd begun to stop being content just me on my own.'

'You—wanted me with you?' she asked breathlessly, starting to believe more and more that it was true, that Jarad, unbelievably, as he said, did love her.

'Believe it.' He smiled. 'So there was I, taking you to

see my folks not once, but twice. Only on the second occasion my cousin Franklin tried to monopolise you.'

'You were jealous of Franklin?'

'Especially when you seemed to enjoy having him drool over you.'

She laughed, couldn't help it. 'That's a bit strong,' she protested, but suddenly realised, 'So that's why you were such a snarly brute!'

'Forgive me, sweetheart. I've never been so affected before—you, my dear, were upsetting *my* equilibrium.' He kissed her then, and gently smiled. 'I did come to check you were all right on that Saturday, when you went to bed without so much as a goodnight, but you wouldn't answer.'

'You knew I was there?'

'I saw a line of light under your door for a few seconds before you put your light out. So I went back to the party, giving myself a lecture on how you were my guest and how I should be making sure you were having a pleasant time. Only…'

'Only?' Merren prompted, thoroughly enthralled.

'Only the next time I saw you with Franklin he was kissing your hand—and you weren't objecting.'

'And you were jealous again!' she gasped.

'Blindingly,' he answered ruefully. 'Do you realise, woman, that I decided never to see you again?'

'You did? When was that?'

'On the drive home. You'd given me more than enough to think about.' Merren remembered that drive home—she'd had enough on her mind too, she recalled without effort. 'You'd captivated my family with your natural charm, and—I admitted—I'd been jealous of my cousin and hadn't liked it, and you'd kissed me better, and I'd definitely liked that. I realised I was on dangerous ground.'

'Which was why you decided you weren't going to see me again.'

'Which is why,' he grinned, 'by the following Saturday I found myself seeking you out here—purely because you'd been in my head all week and I simply just had to give in and see you.'

'I was mowing the lawn,' she recalled dreamily, 'and you stopped by because you don't like telling lies and...'

'And starting lying my head off by inventing that I'd called because my mother might ask if I'd seen you—when in actual fact I wanted to see you—because I needed to.'

'Oh, Jarad,' she sighed, and, loving him with all of her heart, she declared, 'No wonder I fell in love with you.'

Jarad gathered her closer and kissed her lingeringly before pulling back to look tenderly into her shining eyes. 'When?' he asked. 'When did you know you loved me? Do you know?'

'I know exactly,' she smiled. 'It was in the middle of a kiss. You'd gone for my jugular over Franklin kissing my hand, and I'd taken enough, so I kissed you; and my heart started to thump—and I just knew then that I was in love with you.'

Merren reached up and kissed him, and for countless minutes they were content to be close once more, sitting with their arms about each other. Then Jarad was planting loving kisses to the sides of her face and telling her, 'You're a pretty wonderful woman, Merren Shepherd, do you know that?'

'I'm sure you're wrong, but I couldn't be happier that you think so,' she murmured.

'I don't think it; I know it,' Jarad declared tenderly.

'Because I borrowed that money from you?' she asked softly. 'I always meant to pay it back,' she felt she should tell him. 'I was going to get a weekend job and save...'

'Oh, my darling, there was never any need for that!'

'For me there was,' she smiled. 'Anyhow, when Uncle Amos told me he'd put ten thousand pounds in my bank ac—'

'The money came from your uncle?' Jarad questioned.

'You don't sound at all surprised that he has that sort of money!' Merren exclaimed.

'Your uncle has a brilliant engineering brain. From what I saw of some of his work when we were in his workshop, I'd have been more surprised if one or two of his inventions hadn't netted him a fortune.'

'Good heavens!' she gasped. 'How come I never knew? I always thought he was church-mouse-poor.'

'And I thought he must have some gambling vice or other that kept him poor and prevented you from going to him when you were in financial trouble.'

'Oh, nothing like that!' Merren said. 'He's just a super uncle, and, though he's asked a couple of times if I was all right for money, I didn't know he had any so I always let him think I didn't have any money problems.' She paused, and, secure in Jarad's love, felt able to tell him, 'That was until last Monday, when I left you. I was upset and...'

'Aw, come here,' Jarad butted in, just as if he couldn't bear the thought of her being upset. He held her close, and kissed her hair. 'Forgive me, sweetheart. To let you go that night was one of the most difficult things I've ever had to do. But you'd hesitated, unsure about committing yourself to me in our lovemaking, and I knew I had to let you go.'

'You told me to go, to leave—for me? I thought you'd rejected me!'

'Rejected you! Oh, my sweet innocent, I wanted you like crazy. How I was able to let you walk out through that door I shall never know!'

Merren, her colour just a trifle pink, sat and stared at him, then admitted, 'My head's been so mixed up. I couldn't—Monday morning—when you came to my room—it had something to do with me owing you money. Yet, when I came to see you Monday evening— and the money I owed you must have been rattling around in my head somewhere—I never gave money a thought. Do I sound a bit confused to you?' she paused to ask.

'Delightfully so,' Jarad grinned, and she had to laugh. 'But I'm following you.'

'Anyhow,' she went on to confess happily, 'I thought you'd rejected me, and I couldn't help wondering if you'd done it deliberately so I might know what it felt like—only I wasn't very sure about that.'

'I shouldn't have let you go in that state.'

'But you had to,' she said. 'Anyhow, when I'd got myself together again, I knew I was going to pay you back every penny of that money—but I didn't want to see my family again that night.'

'So you drove here to stay overnight with your uncle?'

Merren nodded. 'He could see I was upset, and upset with my family—and I was weak enough to tell him about the money, about you letting me have the two thousand pounds, and you giving my father four hundred— and he guessed that I cared for you.'

'Poor love, I'm glad he was there for you to go to.'

'I still didn't know he had any money,' she confided. 'Anyhow, he made sure I went to bed, and next morning suggested I didn't go to work but went and fetched my belongings and moved in with him—then he went out, and when he came back he told me how the house I'd always thought my father owned belonged to him, that he'd bought it for my mother but kept it in his own name. And how he'd put ten thousand pounds in my bank account, and intended to give Robert ten thousand too.'

'So you straight away sent me a cheque.'

'And you telephoned—as angry as the devil.' She grinned.

'And you made me angrier than ever with your jibe about, "Not by selling my body".'

'I'm sorry,' she apologised prettily.

'I should think so too!' he growled, and held her close, burying his face in a cloud of her hair. And Merren had never known such bliss. Jarad leaned back and looked deeply into her eyes. 'Happy?' he asked softly.

'Blissfully,' she answered.

He smiled, as if it was the same for him. 'Are you going to forgive me for all those times I've upset you?'

'Forgiven,' she laughed. 'Providing...' She broke off, and just had to ask, 'Why did you give my father that money on Saturday and tell him not to mention you had called?'

'Nothing in any way sinister, I promise you,' Jarad assured her. But she was feeling more and more secure in his love by the second, so did not truly need that assurance. But he went on to explain. 'I did it for you, my darling.'

'Me! I didn't want you to give my father money! I wouldn't have wanted you to...'

'I know, my love, which is why I asked him not to mention I'd called.'

She caught her breath in surprise. 'Oh, Jarad. You accused me of deliberately misconstruing your motives. Did I get it totally wrong, as you said?'

'Totally,' he smiled. 'But I'll forgive you.'

She had to smile back, but also had to ask, 'Didn't you think my father would tell me anyway?'

'I judged he'd prefer you not to know, but since I was only helping him out a little because I didn't want you to have to endure any more pressure—I'd an idea you'd beggar yourself to fund him rather than let me do it—I felt it would be better to get his word that you'd know nothing of my visit.'

'One of my nieces gave the game away,' Merren felt she should mention. 'Oh, Jarad,' she cried from the heart, 'you must have hated me and my accusations!'

'How could I possibly hate you? I adore you,' he told her gently, but added good-humouredly, 'I'd admit I did take a dim view of your nerve on Monday when you had the sauce to accuse me of deliberately setting you up for a spot of seduction at Birchwood.'

'I'm a wretch,' she grinned. 'I'll categorically state now that I'm sure your motives were of the purest—but...'

'But?' Jarad prompted seriously, his expression telling her that he wanted nothing lurking in dark corners to worry her.

'I think I've worked it out,' she answered. 'You couldn't tell me you knew I'd be at Birchwood, because to do so would have meant I'd know you'd called at my home—had maybe seen my father and to have been told where I was.'

'Clever girl,' he complimented her, his good humour showing again.

'Why did you come, though—you didn't know then how you felt about me?'

'I might not have faced up to the fact that I am, quite desperately, in love with you, my darling, but you were on my mind the whole time. I'd called at your home because of some compulsion to see you. When I knew where you were heading I knew not only did I want to be with you but, when I argued against that—which, poor attempt though it was, I tried to—I knew I just didn't like the idea of you being all alone at Birchwood.'

'You didn't?'

'Sweetheart, I'd been in the next bedroom at Hillmount when you had a nightmare—I just couldn't bear the thought of you being all alone at Birchwood and having another. I couldn't bear to think of you waking up yelling and frightened in a strange house, with no one there to comfort you.'

Merren stretched forward and kissed him, her heart in her eyes. 'Should I ever forget to tell you, I think you're a pretty wonderful man,' she whispered huskily.

Jarad kissed her, and held her, and they clung together for ageless moments. As Jarad held her, Merren held him—she wasn't dreaming; this was actually happening. And her heart was full to overflowing when he leaned back and, his grey eyes warm and tender on her, breathed softly, 'I love you so much, Merren.'

'And I love you,' she answered. They kissed gently.

Then Jarad, his look loving still, but his tone direct, wanted to know, 'So who's this other man you're always going out with?'

'Other man?' she enquired, mystified. 'Oh, you mean Bertie! Oh, he's just a very good old friend.'

'Nothing more than that?'

'Nothing more, I promise,' Merren assured him, still trying to take on board that Jarad was actually jealous! 'Bertie Armstrong and I have been chums for donkey's years. I can't remember a time when I didn't know Bertie.' What she did remember was what an awful feeling jealousy was, and so was at pains to take any whisper of jealousy away from the man she loved. 'I love you, and only you. Bertie is just a good friend and nothing more. I'll introduce you to him and then you'll see.'

Jarad eyed her steadily for perhaps about five seconds, and then, taking a long-drawn breath, he asked, 'Will we have to invite him to our wedding?'

'Well, he is a good fr...' Her voice failed her as what Jarad had just said came to have greater meaning. Her eyes went huge; she didn't know that she hadn't lost a little of her colour. 'I th-think you've just proposed!' she gasped.

Jarad looked levelly back at her—and seemed strangely tense all of a sudden. 'I know I did,' he answered. 'And right at this minute, while I cling on waiting for your answer, I'm feeling very nervous. So if you could think about it quickly and...'

'Oh, Jarad,' she cried huskily, 'it doesn't need any thinking about.'

Merren stirred and opened her eyes to another sun-filled day on the tropical island. But she saw neither the sun nor the island, but had eyes only for the man who was half sitting up in the same bed, looking gently down at her.

'What time is it?' she asked, marvelling how she could still feel a little shy after they had shared so much.

Grey eyes smiled down at the pink glow on her skin, 'Good morning, Mrs Montgomery,' he answered, and placed tender loving kisses over her face. She adored him. 'Has anyone ever told you you have a most beautiful body?' he asked, purely to make her blush some more, she was sure.

She obliged; he grinned. 'What sort of a girl do you think I am?'

'Perhaps a wife who wouldn't mind...' he held his closed left hand in front of her face '...accepting something that belongs to her.'

Merren stared at his hand and then his face—neither gave a clue. She guessed it was another present. Jarad had done so much for her. He had found a job for her brother within his organisation, and given her so much in the month that had gone by since his proposal and their wonderful wedding two days ago—not least the most beautiful diamond solitaire engagement ring.

He stopped teasing, and opened his hand. And Merren, seeing another ring, quickly sat up, her mouth falling open as she at once recognised the ring she had sold and which had once belonged to her mother.

'Jarad!' she gasped, speechless, tears spurting to her eyes. 'Oh, Jarad.'

'Oh, don't cry' he begged, as if he couldn't bear it.

'How did you...? Where...? Did they...?'

'Are you happy?'

The answer was written on her face. 'Oh, darling!' she cried. 'I didn't know I could be so happy. But—I never thought I'd ever see my mother's ring again. Oh, thank you so much.'

'With my love,' he said softly, and Merren knew herself well and truly loved.

She leaned forward and kissed him, the sheet, her only covering, falling down, her heartbeat hammering with a newly discovered tempo as her naked breasts came into contact with his naked hair-roughened chest. Of their own volition her arms went up and over his shoulders. She felt his left hand come to hold her right breast.

'Unless you especially want to get up now?' Jarad suggested softly.

Merren smiled, pulled back, looked at her loving husband and smiled again, 'I think I'd like to stay here with you for ever,' she said in a whisper—just before he kissed her.

PARENTS WANTED

Families in the making!

In the orphanage of a small Australian town called Bay Beach are little children desperately in need of love, and dreaming of their very own family....

The answer to their dreams can also be found in Bay Beach! Couples who are destined for each other—even if they don't know it yet. Brought together by love for these tiny children, can they find true love themselves— and finally become a real family?

Titles in this series by fan-favorite **MARION LENNOX** are

A Child in Need—(April HR #3650)
Their Baby Bargain—(July HR #3662)

Look out for further Parents Wanted stories in Harlequin Romance®, coming soon!

Available wherever Harlequin Books are sold.

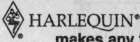
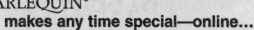

What happens when you suddenly
discover your happy twosome is about
to turn into a...*family?*
Do you laugh?
Do you cry?
Or...do you get married?

The answer is all of the above—and plenty more!

Share the laughter and tears with
Harlequin Romance® as these
unsuspecting couples have to be

When parenthood takes you by surprise!

Authors to look out for include:

Caroline Anderson—DELIVERED: ONE FAMILY
Barbara McMahon—TEMPORARY FATHER
Grace Green—TWINS INCLUDED!
Liz Fielding—THE BACHELOR'S BABY

Available wherever Harlequin books are sold.

HARLEQUIN®
Makes any time special ™

NEARLYWEDS

Almost at the altar—
will these *nearly*weds
become *newly*weds?

Harlequin Romance® is delighted to invite
you to some special weddings! Yet these are
no ordinary weddings. Our beautiful brides
and gorgeous grooms only *nearly* make it
to the altar—before fate intervenes.

But the story doesn't end there....
Find out what happens in these
tantalizingly emotional novels!

Authors to look out for include:

Leigh Michaels—The Bridal Swap
Liz Fielding—His Runaway Bride
Janelle Denison—The Wedding Secret
Renee Roszel—Finally a Groom
Caroline Anderson—The Impetuous Bride

Available wherever Harlequin books are sold.

HARLEQUIN®
Makes any time special ™

Silhouette
bestselling authors

KASEY MICHAELS

RUTH LANGAN

CAROLYN ZANE

*welcome you to a world
of family, privilege and power
with three brand-new love
stories about America's
most beloved dynasty,
the Coltons*

*Brides
of
Privilege*

Available May 2001

Silhouette®
Where love comes alive™